Y0-CPC-015

Visiting for Dollars:

An Annie Barton Series Book

By
Ila Barlow

Strategic Book Publishing and Rights Co.

Strategic Book Publishing and Rights Co.
12620 FM 1960, Suite A4-507
Houston TX 77065
www.sbpra.com

ISBN: 978-1-63135-158-7

To Matt and Jenn

Introduction

It has been said that all creativity is born in our subconscious mind. Distant thoughts come and go when all our defenses are down, like when falling in and out of sleep, when your body is totally relaxed and your mind is allowed to wander. Remembrances surface and yearnings enter into a world that seems real, but is not. We are bathed in a salve manufactured by pure need and it heals us from within.

Chapter One

The office of Attorney Richard D. Mallor is in a crowded downtown office building in a beautiful area of North East, Maryland. It houses not only Attorney Mallor's office, but also the S.R. Watson Dental Office and the Thompson Shoe Repair, which does mighty fine work I might add, and the Butler Bakery. These three businesses are on the first level with the shoe shop being the one in the back and the bakery and dental office out front. You can drop off your shoes, get your teeth worked on, and then stop off at the bakery to warm your soul after the harrowing business of having dental work done, and be on your way. The stairs that lead up to Attorney Mallor's office are around back, next to the shoe shop, with a sign leading the way for first-time visitors. I, however, am mostly a regular. Even though Attorney Mallor isn't the busiest attorney or well thought of, with his strong opinions that some would just rather leave alone, he works at lightning speed, and I like that. No beating around the bush with Richard Mallor; he jumps on an account and gets results within two or three days, and the results are usually good. I refer him to collection agencies and other collection managers all of the time. I like and trust him and so does Pali, and that says a lot, because Pali doesn't like or trust anybody. Pali is my manager and the boss of the Rucker Finance Company where I work. Pali is a small, somewhat scrawny little Italian man who uses Kiwi shoe polish on his temples to hide the gray. We all have come to the conclusion that it is shoe polish due to the shadow around the area (it's real hard to get shoe polish off of skin) and the constant smell of a shoe shop whenever you enter an area where he is. Pali is a great lender and collector, and I'm glad he is the manager of the office in which I work. He does have many sides, however, and we have all learned how to handle them.

We've all been together for approximately three years now and know each other's good sides and bad.

"Go down to Rich Mallor's and pick up the legals on Tom Swank, Annie!" he yells with a growl.

I just stand there looking at him with hands on hips for a good minute.

"PLEASE! Please go to Rich's and pick up the legals! Good God, you might think you were a prima ballerina or something. Christ, what I have to put up with to make a dollar!"

My name is Antoinette Barton, aka Annie, and I've been the collection manager of the Rucker Finance Company and working with Pali for, like I said, about three years. He can be a handful, so we all have learned to just handle him with whatever tools God gave us, and mine are a strong will and a lot of self-respect.

"I'd be glad to, Pali. I'm heading out anyway to visit my friend and yours, Ester Pritten, and she, just by chance, is on the way to North East," I say with a smile and a small pirouette.

"There's a bag with Ethel's shoes in it, too. Take them to Thompson's for new heels . . . PLEASE!"

"Yes," I say after a little hesitation, waiting for the *please*. Pali is also the local undertaker of our little town, and his wife, Ethel, helps with all of the funerals. Poor Ethel must have worn the heels right off those babies walking back and forth helping Pali. They are a kind couple and do a nice service, but that is just one side of Pali, and I think I like that side better than his collector/ lender side, but I'm not perfect by a long shot, so I try to look past the frailties of my friends and coworkers.

"Okay, I'll take Ethel's shoes. Anything else?" *More Kiwi shoe polish?* I think.

"That's it and don't stop at the bakery—my pants don't fit now!" he says with his thumb in his waistband to prove to me that he, in fact, can't breathe well in his pants. Pali has an instinct from hell that I'm sure told him I'd never get past the bakery without stopping. Sometimes it comes in handy, sometimes not.

"Maybe you should buy pants bigger than twenty-eight-size waist," says Hatch.

"You'd look good with a little weight on you, plus we all would love doughnuts."

"No! No doughnuts!"

Within a split second, Edna Mae and Lil are at the door to the backroom at the suggestion of doughnuts.

"Come on, Pali. It's spring! We need to celebrate. You can diet all weekend and get back to your svelte self by Monday morning," says Lil with a wink and a flirtatious smile. Lil is a consummate flirt with all men she works with and many of the male customers she encounters. She's not that great looking, but her attitude and self-assurance exude sex. She has lots of men friends and frequently tells us all about them and their escapades.

I just listen to learn because I have absolutely no experience in this field at all. I never dated a lot in school and have no boyfriend at present. It's probably my thirty-six-inch figure, 12 x 12 x 12. Straight up and down, I have absolutely nothing to work with. I still have freckles. I am, however, pretty tall at five feet, six inches, and I do have great hair, according to my mom, who used to say, "Keep your hair long. It's your redeeming feature, and quite frankly, it's all you have." So there you go. It does have lots of highlights and for that I'm forever thankful.

Now Edna Mae is thirty-something, kind of heavy, blonde, and the person in charge of the front office—make no mistake about it, just ask her! Lil is her helper and just pretty much does as she is told to do. She seems quite competent, but never offers anything extra. She attends to her nails as soon as Pali goes to the bank or elsewhere and keeps pretty quiet except for her sexual escapades, and she shares them often.

Hatch, on the other hand, is very private, saying nothing about his life. Now, between the private silence and his extreme good looks, he most likely has constant action, something I only dream of. Hatch is the office lender and probably the hottest guy in town. He is personality-plus and extremely confident. Who wouldn't be if you looked like that? Sometimes women come in to make a payment and end up drooling on the front counter. It's embarrassing, but we all have learned to just deal with it. I'll find the right guy soon, I'm sure, and I'm just patient enough to wait for him.

"NO, no doughnuts!"

"I'll give you the money, Annie. We need doughnuts," says Edna, getting the petty cash box out of the safe. "It's spring and all!" she says, stuffing a $20 in my hand.

I hear, "Christ, why do I even try?" from the backroom.

"Be back soon," I call as I leave. They all just wave.

Oh, to be free as a bird and on my own on a Thursday morning in the springtime! What a wonderful experience. My car, a 2000 VW sedan, is a little old, but not problematic. It's good on gas, runs well, so what more could I ask for? Ten years old is not bad considering my last car, a 1998 Volvo, had over 250,000 miles on it when it met its demise. It was blown to smithereens when someone didn't like the part-time investigation performed by Hatch and me while looking for the murderer of my friend and customer, Lois Sewellas. I loved that car and still miss it. But the VW will do for now.

The back way to North East, Maryland, is longer, but very

beautiful, and I am really in no hurry. It won't take me long to pick up the legals from Attorney Mallor, chat a while, drop off Ethel's shoes, pick up doughnuts for the gang, and drop by Esther's for a payment. I'll be back by 10:30 a.m. or 11:00 a.m., just in time for more coffee and our goodies.

I park out back at the shoe shop, drop off Ethel's shoes, and make my way up the stairs to Attorney Mallor's office. When I get there, the door is open, so I knock on the glass top of the door to let Mr. Mallor know I am there and walk in. He doesn't have a secretary. Either he won't pay somebody to answer his phone when he has voice mail, or nobody will work for him. I don't know what the story is on that, but for the three years that I've known him and have been sending work out through him, I've never known him to have any help at all. Nobody in the front office, so I call out and just stay there for a while, thinking maybe he is just in the men's room or has stepped outside for a moment.

This part of the office has a desk (*for no one!*), a small leather couch and two chairs, a coffee table with a leather top in the middle, and lots of really nice paintings on the walls, mostly of yachts, small boats, and people on the beach. The water theme is everywhere, including a maritime clock on a side table, old wooden crab nets made into end tables, and wooden oars hanging on the wall. He definitely loves boating, and it's a favorite of many down in this part of Maryland. The clock ticking on the wall is about to drive me to drink, so I decide to just go into the back office and call his name again.

"Mr. Mallor?" I call.

No answer. I can't just walk in and look around, so I wander around the outer office AGAIN, looking at the pictures once more, and all but humming a tune to keep myself company.

I look at my watch and see that it is 10:00 a.m., and I thought I'd be back at the office by 10:30 a.m. or so. This waiting around is messing up my schedule, and the thought of those doughnuts makes me braver.

"Mr. Mallor?" I call louder this time and walk into his back office. No sound at all and nobody around.

"Good grief!" I say aloud. I am sure Pali must have just spoken with him regarding my picking up the legal paperwork on Tom Swank, or he wouldn't have asked me to go get them.

I walk past the desk towards the other room that houses the copier and fax machines and see the bathroom door is open. Now I'm getting pissed, as I don't have time for this delay. When I turn around, I see a foot sticking out from behind the desk. I run around the desk only to find Richard Mallor lying on his side with lots of blood oozing out of his body and running onto the rug, pooling at the edge of the carpet strip. My hand goes to my mouth, and I let out a little yell from the sight of it all. I look all around, not quite clear about what to do at first, but finally find my feet and run like crazy out the door, down the steps, and into Thompson's Shoe Shop, looking for help.

Bud Thompson is at the register when I go in and looks up when the door opens with such force.

"Bud, I need your help! Mr. Mallor is upstairs on the floor, and I think he's dead!" He runs out the door and up the stairs, with me close on his heels. Bud leans down to Mr. Mallor and feels for a pulse on his neck. The look on his face tells it all. Mr. Mallor has been stabbed several times with a letter opener that now lies bloody at the end of the carpet.

"Dear God, what has happened!" Bud says aloud with a visible shiver. He wipes his brow and looks over at me. "When did you find him?"

"Just now. I left shoes with Stan at your place not fifteen minutes ago and came right up here. I stood around for a while because he didn't answer when I called his name, so I wandered back here and saw him lying on the floor with all of that blood everywhere!" I just shake my head and look back at Bud, who is also staring at poor Mr. Mallor.

"I'll call the police. Annie, are you okay?"

"Yes, I'm all right. Are you sure he's dead?"

"I think so," he says and reaches for the phone to call 911.

I, at the same time, reach for my cell to call the office. I know I should ask for Pali, after all, he is the manager, but when Lil answers the phone, all I can think of is Hatch. We had formed somewhat of a relationship about a year ago, and I feel I can rely on him. I'd like it to be more, but that hasn't happened yet. Lil must have told him that I sounded upset because he is immediately on the phone.

"Annie, where are you?"

"I'm at Richard Mallor's office, and he's on the floor with several stab wounds from a letter opener and there's blood all over his carpeting and we think he's dead, Hatch, and I really liked him!" I blurt out.

"Who's we?" he says.

"Bud Thompson, from the shoe shop downstairs."

"I'll be right there!" he says and he hangs up.

"Let's go out to the front office, Annie," says Bud. "Until the police get here." And he takes me by the arm.

"Did you see anybody leaving his office or anything when you were coming up the stairs?" he asks with a concerned look on his face.

"I would have thought of that right away, I think, but I saw no one at all. I was completely alone out in his front office for at least fifteen minutes before I got the nerve to go back into that area," I say, pointing to the back office where Richard Mallor lies dead.

"It couldn't have been long ago that somebody was here because he's still bleeding from those stab wounds. How long does a person bleed like that?" Bud asks, running his hand over his face, visibly shaken.

I didn't know the answer to that question, so I say nothing, but if I didn't see anybody and it has just happened, maybe somebody is still there in the office, and we don't know it.

"What if he's still here?" I say in a whisper that makes the hair on the back of my neck stand straight up. I know the look on my face is of complete horror, because Bud turns an ashen gray. In unison, we get up quickly and make our way to the door. We go down the steps with such speed that I almost lose my shoe and run into Bud's shoe shop just as the first of several police cars arrive with sirens blaring. Not much happens in North East, Maryland, and this is a biggie.

Bud meets the first officer on the scene just outside the door and explains to him that he is the one who called 911.

"Where is the body?"

"Upstairs at Richard Mallor's office. It's Mr. Mallor who's dead!" he says.

"Are you sure?"

"I've known him for the better part of ten years, and I'm sure it's him."

They both run up the stairs followed by three more police officers, and I stay downstairs with Stan, Bud's helper. Seconds later, I see Hatch's car stop out back, and he jumps out at record speed. He runs to the shoe shop and all but rips the door off the hinges coming in. I just stand there looking at him, and he takes me by the hand and pulls me into a warm and protective hug that lifts me off my feet. I just hang there with my eyes closed, feeling the warmth of his body and listening to his quiet strong breathing. After a few minutes, he puts me down and says very quietly, "Tell me what happened, and we'll talk to the police together."

Now, he has me by one hand and is running his other hand very lightly up and down my other arm, probably trying to calm me down, as I am somewhat hyperventilating from what he must think is the unnerving experience of finding poor Mr. Mallor, but in fact, it is from the hug and all of the hand holding and arm rubbing that has me in such a turned-on state, that I could have jumped his bones right there in the shoe shop! Good God, there is something about this guy that makes me completely out of control, like I have never been before. I really need to get a grip.

"Huh?" I say, looking quite confused, I'm sure.

"The dead man upstairs?"

"Oh right, right," I say, pulling myself together somewhat. "It's Mr. Mallor. He's dead, Hatch, and there's blood everywhere and a letter opener on the floor right next to him with blood all over it, so it must be what the guy used to stab poor Mr. Mallor with."

"Okay, we'll talk to the police as soon as they come down," he says, looking up the stairs.

"Let's go up," I say and start up the stairs.

"You sure?"

"Yes, there's an outer office where we can wait. They'll have lots of questions."

We make our way up the stairs, but stay in the outer office while all of the officers and Bud are in the back with Mr. Mallor. The coroner arrives with his team, so the officers start coming out.

"Who found the body?" yells a skinny, young black guy, and I all but leap out of my skin. I hold up my hand, like you do in school—I have no idea why—and say that I did.

"Who are you?" he yells again.

"Annie Barton. I'm with the Rucker Finance Company from Oxford, Pennsylvania, and I came here to pick up some legals."

"Why?" he yells even louder.

Now this guy is getting on my nerves. It has been a harrowing morning. I've been here for some time, and I've missed my doughnuts, and I need more coffee!

"I can hear you without your yelling," I say and stare at him.

The chief walks into the room and stands next to Hatch. I recognize him from Lois Sewellas's house when Hatch and I found her dead in her backyard a year ago while we were out chasing around in the Elkton, Maryland, area.

"Don't I know you two?" he says, pointing back and forth between Hatch and me.

"Ray Hatcher and Annie Barton, Rucker Finance Company," Hatch says, pointing to me and shaking the chief's hand.

"Yeah, Lois Sewellas and that bad state-cop guy," he says, slowly looking back and forth again. "What? Another murder victim, and you're both on the scene again?"

"I can't explain it, chief," says Hatch.

"Is that your name?" yells the first guy again, making me jump yet again. I turn around and give him a dirty look.

"Hollinger, quiet it down. I'll take over now. Get back on patrol, will you!"

"Sure, chief," the loud guy says again and leaves.

Thank God! I think.

"You might want to have his hearing checked," Hatch says quietly, getting a sideways look from the chief.

"What's going on, Adams?" he says to one of the other officers.

"A 911 call came in at ten-fifteen a.m. stating a dead body was found in the office of Richard Mallor at this address. When we got here, Bud Thompson from the shoe shop downstairs approached us outside and said he'd made the call and escorted us upstairs to see the body, which has not been moved yet. We've taken several pictures of the scene, but the ME's office is here, so you might want to go look before they move the body or anything."

"Don't move anything yet!" he bellows to the people in the back room.

Good God, he scares the hell out of me with this, and I wonder what is with all of the yelling in Cecil County.

"Who found the body?" he says, writing in his little tablet. They all have little tablets and are writing in them.

"I did," I say.

"Of course you did!" he says with a head shake. His body language tells me he has little patience with this entire scene and quite possibly with many things.

"I'm doing my job, just like you are, chief, and that's why I'm here!"

"Officer, this is purely coincidental with Annie finding two dead bodies in a year. She doesn't usually do this," says Hatch emphatically.

"I'm glad as hell to hear that, Mr. Hatcher," he says, leafing back through his tablet. "And just why are you here again with Ms. Barton?"

"She called me at the office to tell me there was another dead body, and I came right down to help her out. We work together at the Rucker Finance Company."

"Um," is his only reply.

"How well did you know Mr. Mallor, Ms. Barton?"

"He's our legal representative for the state of Maryland," I answer.

"That's not what I asked you. How well did you know him?" He, too, is getting on my nerves.

"Not real well. I come back and forth to get legal papers sometimes, and I've talked to him on the phone a lot of times, but I talk to a lot of attorneys on the phone about some of our cliental," I say rather arrogantly.

"How long has this attorney been handling accounts for the Rucker Finance Company?"

"About three years or so, hasn't it been, Hatch?"

"I think so."

"What time did you get here this morning?"

"Well, I arrived about nine-thirty a.m. or so and left Ethel's shoes downstairs with Stan to have new heels put on them, as Pali gave them to me this morning when I was leaving to come here, since they were really worn down from all that prancing back and forth that Ethel does helping Pali with all of those funerals he does. And I stayed talking with Stan for a few minutes before I came upstairs to speak with Mr. Mallor to pick up the legals for Tom Swank that Pali told me about. BUT when I got up here, there was nobody at the front desk, but there never is because I'm thinking either Mr. Mallor is too cheap to pay anybody or he's hard to work for because in all of the three years I've been coming down here, there has never been anybody at the front desk, and I don't know why he doesn't just do away with the desk and maybe move the couch over there and make more room for a living room kind of set up here, in case people want to sit down and visit." Hatch and the officer make brief eye contact, but I just go on.

"Now," I continue, "I called his name twice, but he didn't answer, so I figured he must be either in the men's room or he'd just stepped out or something, so I looked around at the pictures and the books in the bookcase and hummed a little tune just to pass the time. I started to get really aggravated, because I wanted to stop and get doughnuts for the staff with the twenty dollars that Edna Mae had given me from petty cash, and I wanted to be back by around ten thirty or so, so we could all have doughnuts and coffee together, even though Pali didn't want me to get them because his pants don't fit."

The chief is just standing there looking at me with a really stupid look on his face, so I look at Hatch and say, "Well, he wanted to have all of the facts!"

"And now he does," he says quietly with a smile. "Not usually like this," he says to the chief.

The chief pauses for a minute and then goes on. "At what time do you think you went into Mr. Mallor's office to find him dead, Ms. Barton?" he says with a sigh and writes something in his little tablet. He seems aggravated and so am I.

"I didn't check the clock!" *Brief pause.*

"At what time do you *think* you went into Mr. Mallor's office to find him dead, Ms. Barton?"

"Approximately ten o'clock. I went back and called his name and went over to see if the bathroom door was closed and when I saw it was open, I turned around to go and saw a foot sticking out from the backside of the desk. I ran around to see Mr. Mallor there with blood running out of the wounds on his chest, and I ran down to get Bud from the shoe shop. We came back up and he determined that he was, in fact, deceased and called 911. He called from here, and I called Hatch."

Bud is standing next to the chief by now, and he starts talking. "We came out here to get away from the back office, and I asked Annie if she saw anybody either here or on her way up the stairs when she came in, since Mr. Mallor's body was still oozing blood. I figured it couldn't have been done too long before. We sat here for a while and then Annie quietly said, 'What if he's still here?' so we ran downstairs. I was scared and so was Annie, and we raced down the stairs."

"I almost lost my shoe," I say and receive yet another stare from the chief.

"It all happened really fast," Bud says.

Both Hatch and the chief have blank stares going on.

"Mr. Hatcher, when did you arrive?"

"Five, ten minutes before we came up here to be with you."

"Are you two involved?" he says, pointing back and forth to each of us.

"Yes," I say.

"No," says Hatch. "We're friends and coworkers," he says quietly.

"That's what I meant," I mutter, looking down at the floor. When I look up again, Hatch has those beer-bottle-colored eyes on me and a little smile on his face, and a flame shoots from my brain to my private parts with alarming speed, and I have to hold onto the chair to steady myself. That darn thing happens a lot! It's a little out of control.

"I'll be in touch. We have all of the information we need here," the chief says and walks away. I guess we are dismissed, so I head for the door.

"Do you want to ride back with me, Annie?"

"No, I'm fine," I say somewhat hoity-toity like, *no, no I'm fine on my own, didn't need that hug anyway . . . just get in your Porsche and drive away, I'll get back in my old clunker of a VW alone.*

I'm pathetic and have no doughnuts!

Chapter Two

I think, with the murder and all, I really shouldn't get the aforementioned doughnuts. But I really could have eaten one or six. I slowly drive back to the office. Hatch has spoken with Pali and gotten him up to speed.

"I just can't believe this has happened again," I say aloud to myself. If I didn't have bad luck, I'd have no luck at all.

Back in Oxford, I park down the street not too far from my new apartment. It's much closer to the office than the last one. A little more expensive, but it's on the first floor rather than the second and is somewhat bigger. Mrs. Schmidt, my last landlady, asked me to move after my previous car exploded in front of her home, causing extensive damage to her neighbor's house and Mrs. Schmidt's porch and lots of siding. I'm sure the insurance company fixed everything, as I still had full coverage on my car, even though it was a 1998 Volvo. It only had a little over 250,000 miles on it, and I loved that car, but the explosion caused irreparable damage, and it was classified a total loss. I slowly walk back to the office feeling a little dejected and somewhat hungry. A look at my cell confirms what my stomach says—it's lunch time. Pali will probably want me to skip lunch since I've been gone since about 9:15 a.m. and it is now 12:30 p.m.

"What, no doughnuts?" asks Edna when I walk in. I just give her a stare and keep on going into the back area to get another cup of coffee and use the bathroom.

I should have stopped at McDonalds for a cheeseburger or Wawa for a Chicken Caesar Wrap—even better. Did I do that? No, no, not me. I'm too conscientious about getting back to work. I'm so busy finding dead bodies I can't even keep track of my own needs. Man, I am in a really bad mood and that is uncommon for me. All of this death and destruction takes a toll on a person. Sipping my coffee, *somewhat burnt* I think, I slip into my desk chair and start looking over the work I have piled on my desk, pre Richard-Mallor dead-person find.

"What! We're not going to talk about this morning?" asks Pali, now on his feet, hands on hips.

"Well, I'm sure Hatch brought you up to speed, Pali. I went to Attorney Mallor's office. He was dead. We talked to the police AGAIN, and now I'm back to work. End of story."

"Okay, we all need lunch. I'll spring for pizza!" Pali adds.

That heart isn't as black as we all thought after all.

"Okay, I still have the twenty dollars from petty cash. We can use that, too," I say.

"We'll eat, talk, and drink Pepsi, how's that?" Pali says, like he is a party planner or somebody. In essence, he is kind of used to putting a luncheon together pretty quickly with his other profession as an undertaker. They can plan really big events and quickly.

"Lil!" he yells, and I almost jump out of my chair.

"Go get pizza and Pepsi. I'll call and order it."

"Works for me. Where am I going?"

Hatch picks up my coffee cup and takes it away to pour down the drain. "Why don't you just take a break until lunch is here?" he all but whispers in my ear.

All I can feel is his warm breath on my neck and the smell of his cologne. That alone is enough to melt my socks. His eyes on mine as he walks past the front of the office glass en-route to the backroom to toss the coffee, is the clincher, and the flame is back, along with a head rush. *Oh my!*

We take our lunch (free, I need to mention again) back to the last deal room that has room for about six or seven people and eat there. We keep our ears open in case a customer comes in. It is determined that Lil is on duty should someone show up. Edna votes to lock the door, but Pali just gives her that look from hell, and it is forgotten immediately.

The pizza is excellent. We hardly talk, just eat, and as I look from one coworker to the other, it strikes me how different we all are and yet how alike.

Pali is a displaced city boy with a wife of the same background and they are now living and working in a small country town. Does she have friends here? Is she happy? Pali works fifty plus hours weekly at the finance company and then there's the other business. He is constantly on the go. When does he give her the time she needs? He seems self focused mostly and really never mentions her at all. Ethel, that's her name. I've never seen her anywhere except at a funeral if I attend one. Maybe she's as nocturnal as Pali seems to be. She also has very black hair. She probably uses Kiwi polish, too. Maybe they're vampires, and now I am squinting to see if he has any of those pointy teeth, when Edna yells.

"That was perfect!" She slaps her hands down on the table, yet again scaring the life out of me and making me jump a foot into the air.

"You okay, Babs?" Hatch asks quietly.

He notices my jumpiness and is probably thinking, *she's about to self-destruct.* He calls me Babs lots of the time. I'm not really sure where that came from, but it seems to be some kind of an endearment, and that's okay with me.

"Yes, I'm good, couldn't be better, and I'm thinking I should get back to work, since the whole morning was wasted in North East."

"Take it easy, Annie, you'll live longer," says Lil.

She should live to be about four hundred because she only has two speeds, and they are slow and slower, I think. She is sucking Pepsi through her straw and has a twinkle in her eye.

"You need to slow down and enjoy life like I do. I like it that way, slow and easy," she says, looking mainly at Hatch.

He is ignoring her as usual, but I blush, remembering some of her stories of escapades between the sheets and on various flat surfaces in and around her apartment. They sometimes confuse me, I'm embarrassed to say, because it shows my lack of escapade knowledge and I only hope one day I can at least relate a little bit. However, it is not at present and that alone puts me in a bad mood in itself. I should listen to Lil. *Life is too short,* I muse. *I could end up like poor Mr. Mallor, dead at a relatively young age. God, I'm pathetic!*

Edna Mae, as Pali calls her, and she hates it because that's really not her name, is a good balance of Lil and me. She can get lots done and also be laid back and relaxed. I envy that a lot. She seems confident, happy, and can be just charming with the customers. It must be Al, her husband. Whenever she mentions his name, she smiles. He is a quiet, kind man and treats her well. She tells us that a lot.

"Al's such a good man," she says. He does this for her or that for her or little things he says shows he really loves her and their relationship is special. I'd be confident and happy too, if I had someone like that.

And then there's Hatch. There's just something about him. It's not his good looks that attract me so much as his way, his concern, his kindness. We're just coworkers. I'd like to be more, but we're not there yet. Now, I say *yet* loosely. We don't really date; we work together and sometimes link up. We're more like buddies. He has never even kissed me, except on the cheek when he stayed for dinner after we'd found one of our customers shot "right between her baby blues," as he put it, and I was a little upset. But I'm an optimist and hope our relationship will progress, and quickly.

"Okay, so now you have two dead people under your belt, Annie. How can that be?"

"Pali, I have no idea. I'm just at the wrong place at the wrong time. Anyway, you sent me down there. Didn't you just talk to him before I left here to go?"

"Yeah, he sounded fine to me."

"Had he talked to you lately about a problem, or did he seem bothered about anything lately?" asks Hatch.

"No, he's been his usual miserable self like always. I never really liked the guy, he's so arrogant and all, but he jumps on these accounts so fast and gets such good results. I hate like heck to start over with somebody else. Guess we'll have to now, though . . ." Pali's words drift off.

"I kind of liked him. He had a real deep voice with somewhat of an accent. I like that in a man," adds Lil.

"You like everything about any man, Lil," says Edna. "Face it, you love men, period!" she says and laughs.

"Well, yeah, I guess I do."

"Okay, okay, this is getting out of hand and away from the necessary discussion about Mr. Mallor."

"Annie, do you think you need some counseling or anything?" asks Pali.

Now he does have a genuinely concerned look on his face, and I appreciate it.

"No, I'm okay. I'm pretty tough, you know," I say with a laugh.

"If you need to take a couple of days off, you can. It's a tough job every day, and now you have experienced two deaths as well. I don't want you going berserk or anything on me."

Now Pali has a smile on his face, and I can see the undertaker side could be quite pleasant. "No, I'm fine, but thanks, anyway, Pali. I appreciate that."

"It's policy! If you encounter stressful situations, you are entitled to two days' of compensation, so take them if you want them."

He is all but yelling, so I think, *Maybe I should take him up on it.* "Okay, I'll take a couple of days! Good grief, I'll get caught up on my cleaning or something."

"You need to schedule a nice massage and get your nails done, Annie, that will make you feel like a new woman," says Edna. "It helps me when I'm stressed."

"Time off will be good, Babs. Take the time and just crash," Hatch says quietly.

"You just need a good tussle in the hay, that's what you need. I could hook you up with a guy I've known for some time now. I'm sure he could accommodate you," Lil adds with a smile and wink as she leaves the room. "Let me know, and I'll call him today," she concludes.

Hatch has a Colgate smile going on and lays his head back with a loud laugh. He just can't contain himself another minute. That Colgate smile of his always makes me smile, too, it's just irresistible, and his eyes are twinkling as well. I don't dare say a thing; I just smile and leave the area. Lil is probably right, but it won't be with her friend. I know who I'd choose, and he has no clue.

Chapter Three

It has been said that all creativity is born in our subconscious mind. Distant thoughts come and go when all of our defenses are down, like while falling in and out of sleep, when your body is totally relaxed, and your mind is allowed to wander. Remembrances surface, and yearnings enter into a world that seems real, but is not. We are bathed in a salve manufactured by pure need, and it heals us from within.

I look at the clock on the nightstand and can't believe it says eight o'clock. I never sleep that late, usually because I'm at work by now. I look around my room and am completely happy. Sunshine is coming in the eastern window, and it makes beautiful colors on the wall as it passes through a cut-glass perfume bottle my Aunt Dell gave me as a kid. I am comfortable, and I stretch and lazily lie there a while. This is a great idea! I must drift off again, because I come to with a jump and am a little confused. I sit straight up in bed and realize that while I was sleeping, I remember something about a guy with long hair and the banging of a door and his jacket with a snake on the back. Was this part of a dream or was it real? Still in a fog, I make my way to the kitchen and put the coffee pot on. What is all of this, and why can't I get it straight in my mind?

I slowly sip my coffee and concentrate, starting to put some of the pieces together. The guy with long hair was on the outside porch at the shoe shop while I was dropping off Ethel's shoes. His jacket had a snake on the back, and it was red on a black jacket. The slamming door was probably Mr. Mallor's door upstairs. That's all of it, but it's better than nothing at all. Why hadn't I remembered it before? Stan had been talking to me, and I just glanced out at the guy for a few seconds, no more. I'm sure now, and I have to let someone know.

I inhale a piece of toast, put on my running shorts, sneakers, and tank top. I'll stop by the office, talk to Hatch, and then get my run in at the cemetery, re-cooping what I just remembered while I run. Running always clears my mind and puts all things into prospective.

"What in the hell are you doing here, you're supposed to be off for two days, and here you are. Girl, you're crazy!" This coming from Lil who we all question on a sanity level, daily.

I walk right past her and whisper, "It's okay, Lil. I'm good, but need a word with Hatch." She just shakes her head. "Hatch," I whisper. He is on the phone, but turns around in his chair, first surprised to see me, then checks me out top to bottom with a slow smile, while continuing his conversation with his customer. I just raise an eyebrow and give him a head tilt.

"I need to see you," I whisper again and point to the counter of the outer office. He nods his head yes and still has that smile going on. I hope all of the running I do strengthens my heart muscle; I'm going to need it just to get through working a few more years with him.

I wait at the counter and am glad that Pali is in a deal room, Lil is on the phone, and Edna is waiting on a customer, so I don't have to explain anything. Plus, I don't want them to hear any of our conversation. Hatch hangs up the phone and comes out to the counter, grinning all the way.

"Couldn't stand to be without me for a day, could you, Babs, and you're looking spiffy in your little running outfit, and I do mean *little*," he says as he leans over the counter, checking out my shorts.

"Listen to me! I remembered something when I woke up this morning, and I don't even know why I hadn't before, but there was a guy with long hair and a jacket with a red snake on it."

Blank stare from Hatch. "Was the jacket on the guy with long hair or just floating around somewhere in a vision?"

"Of course he had it on! It was black and had this red snake on it, and I remember a door slamming, too, possibly the door to Mr. Mallor's office. What do you think?"

"It's more than we had before. We could research it and see where it takes us."

"Come over after work. I'll fire up the computer and see what we can dig up."

"Does that mean for dinner, or should I get sandwiches or something?"

"No, I'll cook. See you later," I say as I make my way to the door, looking back at Hatch, who has a huge smile on his face, probably because of the thought of food.

I run up Route 10 to Maple Street, turn right onto Pine, and enter the cemetery by way of the back entrance. I can put on a few miles here and nobody will care, especially the residents. As long as I stay out of the way of the mowers or diggers, they are happy and so am I. I love it here as it has many mature trees of various kinds. There are several cedars of Lebanon, lovingly grown from seeds by a local resident, which add the special touch to make this particular cemetery very beautiful. It's perfectly maintained by just two people who work daily to accomplish this. Its beauty is renowned.

I have no clue what I'll make for Hatch for dinner, but a pork roast keeps surfacing in my mind. I hotfoot it to the market, pick up said pork loin, and head home. I put a rub together, slather it all over that baby, and throw it in the fridge. Later I'll get it out, put it in a baking bag, and match that with macaroni and cheese, asparagus, applesauce, biscuits with peach jam, and iced tea with lemon and mint. I'll mix up a batch of sauce to pour over the pork, and dinner will be done. I don't have time for an apple pie, but canned filling of some sort will do for a quick pie, probably cherry. He'll love it— what's not to love about that, even if it is canned.

A quick shower and shave, since Hatch is coming over—you never know (wishful thinking on my part)—and a blow dry of my hair. I clean up the house a little, run the vacuum, and fire up the computer to start seeing what I can find out before Hatch gets there. I'll try to compile some data and be ahead of the game so we'll have time to talk, access the information, and possibly make plans to see how we can once again either help the police with their investigation or solve it ourselves.

Chapter Four

Richard D. Mallor was raised in Malden, Massachusetts, a suburb of Boston in an upscale, affluent neighborhood close to the main business center and within walking distance of his schools. He was a quiet boy, a good student, but not outstanding. He was overshadowed by his severely overbearing father, Horace B. Mallor, Esq. He was told every move to make and when to make it, as was his mother, Evelyn Mallor, who took all of the bossing around in stride, but Richard did not. It really pissed him off that the senior Mallor couldn't just let him make his own decisions in life. Even as a junior in high school, he had to start applying to colleges that his dad saw fit for him, rather than where he thought he would like to go. There certainly was no question as to what course he would take: it had to be law and nothing else. He insisted that Richard be a lawyer and someday take over his practice, end of discussion. Richard, unlike his father, who was always in a three-piece suit and casually elegant on weekends, liked to be in a tee shirt and jeans mostly, with a flannel shirt when it was cooler. He liked working on old cars and small motors in the unattached garage they had on the property.

"How are you ever going to get the grease out of those fingernails to be presentable?"

"I'll take care of it, Dad. I have stuff to get them cleaned up."

"I never did this kind of stuff. I don't know why you do!" he said, slamming the door on his way out. He had no idea why that irritated him so much, but it did.

He said nothing to his father, but wanted to say, "Well probably I'm the mailman's kid rather than yours, and I wouldn't blame Mom, 'cause you're a royal prick, who she should have left years ago." But he didn't.

Evelyn was socially busy with this committee or that committee. She just floated in and out. Dinner, possibly picked up on her way home, was always there, and it was always good. She seemed to be in a perpetual good mood. She shared her day with Richard and Horace each night at dinner and seldom asked about theirs, but that was okay. She was content and that made Richard happy.

Horace never talked at dinner. When Richard applied to and was accepted at Pitt, his dad was elated. Not only did the school have an excellent reputation, it had a law school as well. Richard went off to Pitt, did his undergrad and graduate courses there, and never returned to Massachusetts, except for a visit now and then. He met his sweetheart, Emma Lou Rawlins, there, and they returned to her home of Easton, Maryland. He found this town enchanting and fell in love with it immediately. Her parents were divorced, and her dad had a small, but comfortable beach house on Taylor's Island lying nicely on the Chesapeake Bay. For years Richard and Emma Lou spent every weekend at the beach house—with or without her dad—lying in the sun, boating, smoking pot, and making love into the wee hours of the morning and loving it. It was the turning point of his life.

When Emma Lou took off with a merchant marine she met in a bar, Richard was devastated and never recovered. He quit his job and stayed at the beach house for two months, wallowing in self-pity, until Emma Lou's dad threw him out. He never went home to his parents, so he drifted around for about six months doing this or that, whatever he could find, until he realized he could live without Emma Lou and started a recovery process that led him to the North East, Maryland, area. He then met Attorney Earl Smithson at a legal aid seminar and started working part-time for him in his North East office. Richard finally joined Attorney Smithson in his practice and bought out Earl when he wanted to retire. Alone, Richard Mallor was a lonely soul who had a wanton look on his face and an "I wish" on the end of his lips. Lost opportunities, un-kept promises, and a relationship not even close to his expectations, made him a somber and quiet man.

Chapter Five

The pork roast smells great. The mac and cheese is done and getting a little crust on top. I take both out of the oven and cover them in aluminum foil, putting them on top of the stove in the back so the oven will keep them warm. I have the asparagus with olive oil and garlic ready to go in and the biscuits are aligned in the baking pan as well. The pie is done and almost cooled. The table is set with peach jam for the biscuits and the iced tea is ready and waiting. Now all I need is Hatch. Five-thirty and still no Hatch. I put the asparagus and biscuits in the oven and pour the sauce over the pork roast, re-covering it when I hear a knock at the back door.

"Pali left the office with me, so I had to take a detour into town on foot, and come around back so he wouldn't see me. My car is out front just down from your place."

"Do you think he thought you were coming here?"

"No, I don't think—" Hatch stops mid-sentence and looks around the kitchen, nose up like a bloodhound. "What's that smell?"

"Oh, I made a pork roast and—"

"Is that a cherry pie!" He is wandering from item to item, checking under covers, smelling each, and smiling at me in intervals.

Good God! What a child!

Pulling himself together, he says, "I got a bottle of wine while running by the state store on my way. Can I open it now?"

"Yeah, I hope it's better than that lousy red stuff labeled wine I had the last time."

"Oh that . . . yes, that was interesting," he says with that Colgate smile while uncorking his bottle and getting glasses out of the cabinet.

He makes himself at home right away here and did as well at the other apartment. I like that, because it tells me we are comfortable around each other. I made myself at home at his house when we ended there after our last big adventure that almost landed us both in the hospital and real close to jail. Hatch was so beaten up from several encounters with some very rough characters that night. I was a bit tussled around, slammed into a springhouse, and almost buried in mud. We did, however, survive and solved the mystery of who killed Lois Sewellas and why. We both felt good about that and the fact that we both lived to tell the tale, and now here we are again. We need our heads examined!

"Hatch, take off your coat and tie. Get comfortable," I say, while putting the pork on a plate and cutting a couple of slices.

"Watcha got in mind there, Babs?" he says, while looking at me over his wine glass with those beer-bottle-brown eyes.

I laugh out loud and say, "Nothing at all. Just sit down and enjoy the meal, it really looks good. You're terrible." I laugh again. It's odd how half a glass of wine can give you such confidence to deal with things. Normally, I'd have dropped the biscuits or something, but with a little vino, I am just fine, relaxed, and can handle it. It is definitely the nectar of the gods.

We eat, and Hatch makes appreciative noises throughout the meal.

"That was a killer of a dinner, Babs! Killer!"

I just gloat and say, "I know. I love to cook!"

"Now, let's get down to business. I think we need a plan regarding this guy with the jacket."

Previously I had typed "red snake on black jacket" in the search area and gotten lots of advertisements for just that from various stores. I looked at all of them but found nothing that really resembled what I remembered of the jacket worn by the guy with the long hair.

"Was the guy young?"

I look out of the window reflecting on that fact. "I don't know really. I didn't see his face, but he struck me as being young, maybe because of the way he moved."

"That could be," says Hatch, taking another drink of his wine. "You never heard a motorcycle or anything?"

"I don't think so." I look up motorcycle insignias and can find no logo that is even close to the snake on the jacket.

"How about gang logos?" Another sip of wine.

This brings up lots of tattoos, flags, hats with small brims, and, on the last page, lots and lots of jackets, usually leather with symbols on them and even snakes. They seem to be from every state. Who knew there were so darn many? Several look good, but I'm not sure they are the same. This is really hard.

"I'll call Stan. Maybe he remembers something, although he didn't say anything when he was questioned the other day."

"What's right around the law office on that street?"

Blank stare from me. "Well, I think a few more businesses. It's mostly a commercial area, but to tell you the truth, I really don't know."

"We need to take a road trip."

Uh oh, not again. "Oh, boy, I don't know, Hatch, we just got out by the skin of our teeth."

"Yeah," he says, looking at the floor.

A smile comes to my face when I remember the excitement of our previous adventure together, and I look up and say, "But it was fun, wasn't it?" My smile widens.

"Yes, it was, Babs, and I'm willing to take another shot at it, how about you?" Now that twinkle in his eyes is like a kid on Christmas morning, and I can't help but laugh.

"Tomorrow's Saturday, we could start with Bud and Stan and go from there."

"Okay, tomorrow it is." We are so excited!

We clean up the dishes, talk, and laugh about our last adventure, especially Hatch's run-in with Dutch beer that totally licked his butt. We laugh and talk for about an hour and finally decide to call it a night.

He leaves with an, "I'll see you tomorrow," finale. He jogs to his vehicle. I watch from the living room window as he eases himself into his little car and slips away into the night.

Chapter Six

Charles Mahan's office is on Marsh Street on the outskirts of North East, Maryland. His auto body shop has been in operation since the 1960s when his father, Hub—Charles senior—opened it. It has operated for forty-five years now. When Dad retired junior Mahan took over. It is a very well-run and well-thought-of business that everyone uses, and it is profitable. Hub still sits on the board of directors at the Riverfront Bank since he has lots of money there. He is a major stockholder as well. Several times, he has shared inside information regarding real-estate deals that had been discussed at those board meetings, and Charles Jr. has played on that information anyway he can to make money. Hub never knew this and wouldn't have approved if he had known, as he was as straight as an arrow and completely trustworthy. His son, Charles, however, is not. His only interest is in making money anyway he can within the guidelines of the law, even if it means bending those laws a little to make it happen. He has connections and uses them. He can gather other businessmen who have money to invest, and they have had several dealings in the past, mostly successful. Charles has no interest in taking over his dad's place on the board—ever—as it will curtail his investment opportunities drastically. Federal regulators examine board members as well as employees, and he would surely get caught making deals with the inside information he has direct access to, but through his dad, it seems to work okay so far.

The large tract of land known as the Marshall Deal at the bank has much promise. It sits right off I-95 and provides access from both north and south to those interested in coming. A large developer has approached the Riverfront Bank regarding developing this tract of land for a major mall, a bank location that could be a branch for Riverfront, and three commercial sites that could mean large fast-food-restaurant chains, and some major rental income for this developer. It is, however, a little narrow, and the developer needs more land to complete this project, which they almost guarantee will be a success. When Charles hears this from his dad, he quickly runs to the Amish farmer whose land adjoins the Marshall tract and offers him an astronomical figure to sell him the thirty-five acres he needs to re-sell to the developer. Astronomical to the farmer, but Charles knows he can re-sell it to the developer for four times as much. Money is bound to be made.

This purchase puts too much of a burden on Charles alone, so he brings in two other businessmen he had former dealings with and talks them into coming up with the cash, guaranteeing them big returns. This puts a lot of pressure on Charles, but they have been successful in the past, and they have no fear in taking a chance again. Richard Mallor sits on the zoning board with Charles Mahan for both Northrup and Windsor townships where the Marshall tract and the extra thirty-five acres lie. When Richard Mallor votes "no" for the development of the property, especially the thirty-five acres Charles Jr. and his cohorts purchased to be added to the original tract, Charles is instantly irate.

It seems a small bird sanctuary has sprung up just off of a tributary of the Chesapeake Bay where several species of ducks, osprey, and blue heron have started to gather at a quickly growing rate. Richard Mallor is a nature lover and also the only one on the board who thinks this area must be saved and protected. This does not sit well with Charles Jr. at all. He now sees the threat of losing all of his investment, plus that of his business associates. The guarantee he had made to them and his wife is being challenged.

"You can't be serious, Richard, there are dozens of those small sanctuaries all along the Chesapeake Bay area, surely this one could be sacrificed!" Richard doesn't see it that way at all, and the turmoil begins.

Charles Jr. feels his blood pressure rising, and he knows the vein in his forehead has started to redden and pulse. He feels it, so he knows others can see it, especially Richard Mallor.

Richard loves this stuff. Having the upper hand always gives him a rush and the game is on. The other side of him floats back to those days and very long and lazy nights with Emma Lou on the banks of the Chesapeake Bay, and he needs to recapture that time through this small sanctuary in his mind. He will never change his mind and he makes that quite clear.

Charles leaves the third and final zoning board meeting mad as a hornet. He goes to his office rather than home to make some phone calls and takes steps to change this divided discussion and make possible the approval of the plan. He just doesn't know how or where to start. He pulls out his bottle of Jack and, with shaky hands, splashes too much into a glass. He is a wreck. How can this happen. He hates Richard Mallor and all he represents. He is probably knee deep in money, but Charles is not, and his wife spends like a drunken sailor!

"Scotty, it's Chuck, we're still in trouble."

"I thought he would come around. You told me the other guys on that board would take your side on this, and it would all be over with now!"

"Look Scotty, we need a majority on this, and the two that are hedging are Rich Mallor and Norman somebody, I don't even know his last name, but he's a bunny hugger and sees Mallor's side because of that. He could be swayed in our direction if Mallor was out of there."

"We have to make this happen no matter what. We have too

much at stake here, Chuck. I can't lose this kind of money and neither can Ed."

"This really presents a problem."

"I know, but just what in the hell do you suggest?"

He should have had more dinner, or not as much in that glass, but his stomach is feeling the effects as well as his head. Nancy has probably made a nice dinner like always, but he was running late from work and couldn't be late for the board meeting, so he grabbed some crackers at a vending machine. This whole thing has been weighing so heavily on him for weeks and he so hates it! He just wants it done and done his way. He sucks down about half the glass of Jack Daniels and takes a deep breath; he hasn't been this upset and worried in a lifetime.

"You know, Ed has connections that could take care of this," Scotty says quietly, like no one should really hear those words.

"How . . . what do you mean?"

"I mean, like eliminating this Mallor guy so we can get this all done."

"You mean from the board? He has to fill out his term and that's another year."

"No, Chuck. Don't be stupid! I mean eliminate him all together. It can be done and very easily."

Charles Jr. doesn't know what to say. He is getting in over his head now, and the hair on his arms stands up from pure fear.

"This is a lot more than I ever bargained for, Scott. I'm not real comfortable with this."

"How comfortable will you and the wife be if you lose all of that money? I'll call Ed and call you back," he says and hangs up.

Chapter Seven

My alarm sounds at 6:00 a.m., and I almost jump through the ceiling, my nerves are still shot! I slept like a dead person, so I'll make it through the day with no problems. I'm one of those people who requires at least eight hours of sound sleep. I brush my teeth, pull my hair up into a ponytail, throw on my shorts and tee shirt, and head out for a run. Back to the cemetery, as it provides me with a good two-mile run on a route I'd mapped out. The morning is crisp, and I feel a little chilly, but know I'll run it off soon. The dogwoods are just starting to blossom, and you can see which ones are going to be pink and which ones white. Running lifts my spirits and sets me up for the entire day. I'll do my two miles, take a shower, and make some kind of breakfast since I can guarantee Hatch will show up for the day having had something like a Pop Tart, or worse—nothing. Several others are out running or walking their dogs. This is a nice quiet little town, just like thousands all across the country. I love living here as opposed to a city.

A shower feels best after a good solid run. I dry my hair, put on jeans, a blouse, and sandals. I lay out a small jacket and scarf to dress it up a little, since Hatch is always dressed elegantly casual. The jacket and scarf will put a little extra to the basics. Then I throw myself into some kind of breakfast. Coffee is a given and the first thing I address. Eggs for the long haul, I always say, so I think I'll scramble up lots with cheddar cheese. I'd pick up a pack of soy-sausage patties. He'll never know if I don't mention it. There are sticky buns and pumpkin muffins in the freezer that I'd made weeks ago, which I had laid out to thaw before my run. Orange juice from concentrate. He'll love it, and I love to eat!

The sausage is cooked, eggs whipped and waiting for Hatch, and the buns and muffins are thawing. I take my coffee out to the front porch to sit and wait.

Now, the porch on this old house is immense, so I thought I'd make the most of it. I have two dark wicker love seats and three chairs. They don't all match, but are similar. I've spray painted one of the love seats and one chair, which I picked up at a yard sale right after I moved in, in the same dark brown as the others. They are different in design, but now are the same color. The others were provided by the landlady, who said I could do anything I wanted with the porch. It turned out so good, that I find not only the landlady, but other tenants here many times, so I know it's a hit that all of us are enjoying. I found a bolt of fabric at the Neighborhood Services Thrift Store and covered cushions I also got there, or made from foam, and covered all of the seats. Then I got similar fabric in prints and stripes to cover pillows that I placed on all of the furniture to make it look comfortable. A couple of small blankets are always thrown over an arm or on the back. A couple of tables with flowers, two hanging pots with ferns, and the look I like is complete. I'd much rather be outside than inside, and I can sit here, watch traffic, talk to neighbors walking by or co-tenants, and just drink coffee and wait for Hatch. It's a happy place for me, and I am just contemplating the need for a rattan rug when I see his car pull up.

Now his 911 Porsche is the only car he has so we usually take mine, since we just want to blend in when we are out collecting information, not become a spectacle for lots of people to remember. I've already gassed up my car in preparation for today. As I'd guessed, Hatch has on jeans, sandals, and a very fitted black tee shirt with a tan jacket thrown over his shoulder, sunglasses, and that Colgate smile. He is looking fine this morning, and my heart takes one of those little leaps that makes me jump just to keep up.

"Well, now, don't you look comfy," Hatch says to me.

"I am, and in my favorite space," I say with a smile. "Coffee?"

"I thought we'd get something on the road."

"Come in, it's all made."

"Really?" he says with that always-amazed look of his.

"You know I love to eat, so I fixed a little something. Come in, we'll eat and get on the road."

"You never cease to amaze me, Babs."

He says that a lot. "I know, it's a gift." I scramble the eggs, nuke the sausage to warm it up, along with the muffins and sticky buns, and breakfast is on.

"How do you do all this and so fast?" he states, standing in the middle of the kitchen, looking around in awe.

"Organization. Sit down here and we'll feast."

The kitchen is not very big, but it is square, so I put a butcher-block table in the center to use for an island. I put a small table and two chairs at the window. I made a really full curtain and covered cushions for the chairs with some of the plaid fabric from the thrift store that I used for the porch pillows, and it looks pretty nice if I must say so.

We eat, drink more coffee and orange juice. (I'll probably have to stop and pee halfway down the road.) We put all of the dishes in the sink to soak until I get back. I put on my jacket, brush my teeth, assemble the scarf, check myself in the wall mirror, and head for the door. Hatch is already on the porch talking with the neighbor.

"Hi, Ellen! How are you and your son doing?" I ask. Ellen is the second-floor tenant and a single mom. Probably around forty or so, and her son, Billy, is ten.

"We're fine, Annie. How about you?"

"I'm good. You remember Hatch, don't you, one of the men I work with?"

"Oh, yes. Are you off to work on a Saturday?"

"Well, yes, doing a little legwork," Hatch says. "Good seeing you, Ellen. Tell Billy I said hi and to keep practicing that pitch of his."

"I will. Thanks. See you later."

Hatch spent one afternoon with Billy throwing a baseball around a few weeks ago when he helped me once again move my furniture from one spot to another. It had been in storage after the explosion and subsequent eviction from my first apartment to this current location. He helped me again and stayed for lunch. I spent one-third of my income on food. It was, however, cheaper than a moving van.

"Let's start with Stan, like we talked about and then work our way down the street, what do you think?"

"Sounds good," I add with a smile.

There couldn't have been a prettier Saturday morning than today. I can see dandelions springing up in yards as we drive by on our way back to North East. I always take back roads if I can, just to enjoy the scenery, and by the little smile on Hatch's face, he loves the back route, too.

"Now, Babs, how do you want to approach this questioning today?"

"You know Stan, don't you? He's small, kind of scrawny, and has crooked teeth," Annie said."

"I don't mean Stan, I know Stan, I mean, when we start to question and speak with the surrounding businesses?"

"Hum."

"We can't do the census thing again, that wouldn't fly."

"Yeah, I mean, no, and we're just never going back to Edgar's with his Dutch beer," I say with a wide smile.

"Stop!"

"Okay, we'll come up with something."

"That's what I'm trying to do now."

"You are so intense. We'll just wing it as we go."

"We can't just wing it. We have to have a plan like we did before. You have to admit we were pretty good with the census line, and people really cooperated with us."

"Yeah, they did, and I had fun like I've never had fun before. I loved it and all of the excitement," I gush with a smile. It doesn't take much to amuse me. I live a really boring life.

"I know you did, Babs. It showed."

"And now here we are again. I'm so excited," I say with a laugh.

"Don't get too excited. if Pali gets wind of this, he'll have a fit."

"He'll never know!"

"Right."

I pull into the back parking lot at the shoe shop and get out, with Hatch right behind me. Stan is at the register and there are no customers.

"Hey, Annie, how are you doing?" he asks as we come through the door.

"I'm good. You remember Ray Hatcher from Rucker's, don't you, Stan?"

"Yeah, you came down the day Rich Mallor was found, didn't you?" he says and reaches out to shake Hatch's hand.

"Yes, I did Stan, good to see you again."

"You, too."

"You know, Stan, when I got home, I remembered something that I hadn't thought of that day and wanted to run it by you," I say.

"Okay."

"When I dropped off Ethel's shoes, I remembered hearing a door bang and I glanced over to the side door there and saw a man with long, blondish hair wearing a black jacket with a snake on it."

"You did?"

"You don't remember seeing him or hearing a door banging?"

"Not really."

"Hum, I was hoping you had."

"Does a black jacket with a snake on it mean anything to you? I mean, from this area, maybe a club or gang or anything?" Hatch adds.

"Nothing."

"Well, I just wanted to run that by you. Thanks, Stan. Any information on the Mallor murder at all?"

"Well, according to the local paper, there are no leads at all. It said in yesterday's paper that there were no suspects and nobody in custody. You know, he was a strange bird, but I kind of liked him."

"Me, too, I'll miss coming down here to see him and you guys, too," I say.

"Yeah, maybe they'll get this resolved and it can all be put to rest soon."

"Did you know him well? Was he involved with any organizations or clubs around here?" Hatch asks.

"Did anybody know Richard Mallor?" Stan says with a slight laugh. "He pretty much stayed to himself and was a quiet, strange kind of guy. Sat on the zoning board for this township, and I think the next one, too."

"Really? Had he been on that board long?"

"Yeah, and they were feuding like crazy because there's a big developer trying to get plans approved for a pretty good size mall just out of town. Now the tract itself isn't wide enough, but there was an additional thirty-five acres that was being added on, and Mallor opposed this because there's a bunch of ducks or geese and other critters that settled on a stretch of that land and he wanted it to be a preserved area."

"So the developer can't get the plan through without that piece?"

"Right. The original piece is too narrow without the additional piece to pass all of the specs for roads within it, and I heard Charlie Mahan bought that extra piece from an Amish farmer about six or eight months ago so he could re-sell it to the developer. Paid the Amish man dearly for it, from what I hear."

"Hum, so Mallor was the only opposing member on that board?" asks Hatch.

"That's what I hear. Could be wrong on that, but it didn't get passed and caused a lot of friction within the board."

"Who's Charlie Mahan?" I ask.

"He and his dad, Hub, have the auto body shop about three streets over. Been there for years, and they do real good work, are the busiest in the area. Hub sits on the board at the bank."

"What bank is that?"

"Riverfront over on Market Street."

"Heard they were going to have a branch in that mall along with lots of fast food places and all," said Stan.

"Who's the Amish man?"

"Stoltzfus. Don't know his first name. I'd think that piece of land would be too marshy, though, being so close to that tributary there off the Chesapeake, you know, but heard the developer had no problem with that at all."

"So it's real close to a stream that runs in the bay?" I ask.

"Yeah. The Amish man has been farming it for years, but raising corn or whatever on a piece of land and putting up buildings are two different things altogether, you know?"

"Yeah, marshlands aren't too stable as a rule," Hatch responds.

"Well, we just wanted to come down here and talk to you about this stuff."

"You want Ethel's shoes? They're done."

"Oh, yeah, I'll take them. How much do I owe you?"

"Twelve-fifty. I'll put them in a bag."

"Take care, Stan. Keep us abreast of any information that might come up. Just call the office."

"Will do, take care."

We leave, Ethel's shoes in hand.

"Well now, it sounds like that piece of land could be a sticky wicket for the developer and one he would want settled ASAP," I say.

"And, even more for that Mahan guy who bought the extra piece from the Amish man, 'cause I'm sure he wanted to re-sell it fast and for a small profit."

"Yeah," I say, pondering the facts.

"Let's get coffee. We have to think," Hatch says, hurrying to the car.

"You want more coffee after all we had at the apartment?" I say, astounded.

"Well, yeah. We have to talk this out with all of the facts laid out before us!"

"Okay."

"There's a diner about a block down the street on the other side. You want to walk?"

I nod my head yes and say I'll throw Ethel's shoes inside while Hatch goes in to ask Stan if we can leave the car there while we go to the diner. There are at least fifteen spots in the lot, so it shouldn't be a problem, but it's nice to ask.

We sit in a booth, and before I have my handbag down, two waitresses are at the table poised for orders. They look at each other, one finally slinking away in defeat. I'm used to this, Hatch is a chick magnet, and they fall all over him.

"How can I help you?" she says with a wide smile.

Hatch just smiles and looks at me to order first. She is still ogling Hatch, and when I say I'll have coffee, she jumps and looks over at me, like I just appeared from thin air. She clearly hadn't seen me before I spoke, but, like I said, I'm used to this while in Hatch's company.

"Oh, okay, and you sir? What can I get for you?"

"Coffee would be great for me, too," he says and gives her that Colgate thing.

I think I hear her sigh as she leaves. "Good God!" I say.

He just winks and smiles at me. He knows.

"Now we have some facts!"

"What facts?" I say.

"Babs! Richard Mallor sat on the zoning board for an area that has some major development pending, but it sounds like he screwed things up with his disapproval because of the wildlife activity on that little tributary. I'm thinking that guy, that Mahan guy, who bought that other piece of land from the Amish man had big plans for a resale, a big time resale."

"Yeah, and it sounds like his dad sits on the board at the bank, and he probably knew about the development plan and probable loan through the bank and now this no vote from Mr. Mallor has thrown a monkey wrench in his plans."

"It sounds like Sonny is getting inside information and acting on it. I'll bet he would double his investment selling that tract of land to the developer and that could be reason to want to eliminate R. Mallor Esq. from the zoning board." He wiggles his eyebrows up and down.

"Man, you are good," I say. "I wish we knew who the Amish man is or where the land is."

"All that stuff is at the courthouse and is public record, so we'll go there and ask."

"Wait a minute! You're right. I think if we go to the recorder of deeds office or land transfer section, we'll find what we want, and then we'll know where the property is and can go there and talk to Mr. Stoltzfus."

"They aren't going to let us just wander in and look around with no good reason, though."

"Hum," Hatch says while drinking his coffee. He smiles and says, "How about, because we work for the finance company, we're researching property for loan solicitation for a better rate?"

"Would that work?"

"Beats me, but it's worth a try. However, the courthouse is closed on Saturday."

"Rats!"

"We'll come back on a weekday."

"How do you propose we do that when we work together and cannot take the same day off?"

"One of us has to do it," he says.

"I have two days yet. I could come down on Monday, check out the records, see what I come up with, and then we'll go to this Stoltzfus guy and talk."

"It's a plan!"

"Okay, I'm going to hit the ladies room, and we'll start with the businesses around Mallor's office."

"I'll be out front."

My sixty-four ounces or whatever of coffee has kicked in, and a camel I'm not. I have to hit the bathroom *now*. I redo my makeup, brush my teeth, retie my scarf, and just generally spruce up. Lipstick, lip gloss, a little hair spray, and I'm ready for anything. There is a newspaper on the counter as I leave the bathroom, and our cover is complete.

"Let's go back to the car. I have tablets in the back seat!" I say, walking at a dead run.

"What for?"

"Our cover! We're reporters from the *Baltimore Star*, and we're compiling information about the murder of Richard Mallor for an article," I smile widely. "What do you think?"

"I like it! I like it a lot, Babs." And he just winks at me.

We hike back to the VW, each grab a tablet and pen from my stash, and look around for our first victim.

"The bakery!" says Hatch.

"No! I refuse to go to the bakery!"

"Well, just why is that!" he says somewhat perturbed.

"My pants are too tight now. I don't mean to sound like Pali, but I can feel a difference, so I won't go there because as soon as I smell all those doughnuts and baked goodies, I'll cave and lose control. I'm not going!"

Hatch takes off his shades, leans his head to the side, and checks out my hindquarters. "You look the same to me, and it's not bad there, Babs. I don't think a doughnut or six would hurt you, and you know you can't stop at just one."

"Come on, we'll start with the dentist's office. Just give them that Colgate smile of yours, and I'm sure they'll tell you anything you want to know."

"Good morning. What time is your appointment?" asks the older lady behind the counter surrounded by glass windows. Her teeth look like they haven't been cleaned in years! *How could that be, working for a dentist? You'd think she'd get all of the free cleanings she needed, for God's sake!*

Hatch flashes his pearly whites, and she seems to drift into a mild trance.

"We're from the *Baltimore Sun*," he starts.

"Star! Star!" I frantically whisper behind him.

"Oh, I mean Star, the *Baltimore Star*. I'm new to this paper and sometimes I get my constellations mixed up," he says with a little laugh and a Colgate special. "We work for the newspaper and need to ask you some questions regarding the recent murder of Attorney Richard Mallor, whose office was upstairs?" He ends with a question, and his head nodding in a yes manner.

Now she is still in that trance mode, so the confusion of the name of our paper flies right over her head. Her eyes are fluttering, and, for a brief moment, I think she might take a header onto her desk, so I step in.

"My name is Malorie Winston, and I'm the assistant editor with the Star and if you could give us just a few minutes of you time, we'd appreciate it." She seems to revive a bit, looks over at me, and gives a little sigh, clearing her throat. Glancing back at Hatch, she fixes one side of her hair a little and pats her chest, trying to get her heart beat regulated a little, I'm thinking, and get somewhat pulled together.

"Whew! What did you want to ask me and where are you from?"

AGAIN! "We are from the *Baltimore Star* newspaper doing an article on the mysterious murder of Attorney Richard Mallor, whose office was upstairs. Is there anything you can tell us about Mr. Mallor that could shed some light on why anybody would want to murder him?"

She squints at the ceiling a bit, I guess contemplating my question.

"Well, no. I certainly wouldn't know anything about that. He seemed like a nice man and had really great teeth, you know?" she says, looking up at me with a pathetic gaze.

"Okay." I write "pathetic" in my official tablet.

"Did he seem busy? I mean, did he have a lot of clients coming and going on a regular basis?"

"A lot of people park out front and make their way around the side, but lots of folks don't know there's a lot out back and they could be heading back to the shoe shop instead of up to see Richard . . . that's what I called him, Richard," she says with a little giggle while she fumbles with her necklace.

Oh my! "Were you two friends?" I ask with a suggestive smile.

"Oh, my no. He doesn't even know my name probably, or didn't know my name, but he was a handsome devil, and sometimes when he'd park his Lincoln out front here, he'd wave to me as he walked by. He had his teeth cleaned every six months religiously!" she finalizes.

"So, you don't know anybody he hung out with or anything?"

"No, he just waved and went on. When he came in for his appointments, he would just read the paper until his turn came around and I called his name."

"Okay. Is Dr. Watson in this morning?"

"No, he said he needed the weekend off. We have a fill-in dentist here this morning for emergencies only. He's usually in our Havre de Grace office, and I don't think he really knew Richard."

"So Dr. Watson is not in until Monday?"

"Tuesday," she says quickly. "He wanted a long weekend, you know?" She purses her lips and seems to want to say more, but is hesitant.

"Is there something wrong with Dr. Watson or something?"

"Well," she says and looks both left and right. "You didn't hear it from me, but he's having an affair with a much younger woman, and I don't think that's right! She's at least twenty years younger and looks like a floosy, you know what I mean?"

"Uh huh," I reply, thinking, *it's time to go.*

"I mean, his wife's a royal bitch, but at least she's his age! If he wanted other female companionship, I'd have been more than willing to accommodate him, if you know what I mean." She ends with that same pathetic look of hers.

I turn around to find Hatch checking out the old dental utensils that Dr. Watson has on display in a case. He has an agonized look on his face and is holding his jaw.

"We should go now, Mr. Williams. We are close on time."

"Right, Ms. Winston."

"Thank you for your cooperation," he says with a smile, and we quietly leave the office.

"She's pathetic!" I say quietly. "Tell me if I ever get like that, will you?"

"All righty, Babs. Who's next?"

We stand on the sidewalk and look around. "We should have asked a couple of the waitresses in the diner. He must have had lunch there—it looks like the only close place to go for lunch." We continue looking around, noting a jewelry store across the street, a used bookstore, some kind of water testing office, and a Laundromat.

"Nothing looks real promising here. How about the residential area past this strip of offices?" Hatch says, looking up and down the street.

"Okay, we'll stick with the reporter line. How's that sound to you?"

"Pretty darn good, Miss Winston. Lead the way," he says as he puts his hand on my back to get me across a stretch of sidewalk that leads back to the apartment house first in line. Now I love when a man does that with his hand on either your back or elbow, indicating a protective presence. I look over at him and smile slightly.

"What?" he says quietly.

"Nothing," I say and keep on walking. He knows; he just loves to make me simmer.

The apartment house looks like it has only two units. It does have a security entrance, however, so I ring the buzzer, hoping we'll have luck getting in. No one answers, so I ring it again.

"Hello?" is the response.

"I'd like to speak with you for just a minute," I say into the intercom.

"Who are you?"

"We are with the *Baltimore Star*, and we'd like to ask you some questions regarding Richard Mallor, the attorney next door, could you talk to us?"

No response. I turn around to go to the next unit when the door unlatches with a click, and Hatch quickly grabs the handle. We make our way into the hall that leads back to the interior door. It is the worse set up I'd ever seen in any apartment house yet. The hall leads to the very corner of the area, and the door is all but wedged into the far right corner. I hear commotion coming from within, and the door opens. A young woman appears with a smile on her face. That is a good sign.

"You need help with something?" she asks.

"Yes, thanks," says Hatch.

"We're from the *Baltimore Star* looking for any information we can gather on the mysterious murder of Attorney Richard Mallor right next door. I'm Malory Winston, and this is Tom Williams." We all shake hands.

"I'm Melissa Banks," she says smiling, and I notice she has a gap between her front teeth you could drive a Buick through!

"I'm sure you heard about the murder of Attorney Richard Mallor right here in this small strip mall, haven't you?"

"Well, yeah, everybody knows about that!" she says.

"Did you know Attorney Mallor?"

"No, but he did my brother's divorce, and *she* got everything. Absolutely everything!"

Melissa is a large woman, completely dressed in Spandex, and I am really hoping it is of good quality, because it is stretched to the max, and I have a feeling I should hold my breath or something.

"Mommy! Mommy!" we hear from behind her, and three little girls come running to see who is at the door, peeking past her legs at us. All I can see are three little curly-blonde heads.

"Go watch cartoons!" she bellows. "God! Kids suck the life right out of you!"

"I don't like that one!" the smallest one says.

"I do, and she wants to turn on Sponge Bob, but I hate Sponge Bob," one kid says teary.

"Hate is a pretty strong word for Sponge Bob!" the mom says.

"Okay, I don't like Sponge Bob!" the teary one said correctly.

"That's better, now go watch something while I speak with these nice people." The little ones scurry away, and she gives a heavy sigh.

"Have you heard anything from the neighbors or anybody about this murder? We're compiling facts for an article."

"I really don't know anything about Mr. Mallor. I've never met him. Like I said, he did my brother's divorce and that's all I know. Sorry I can't help you."

The girls are fighting over the TV again and she says, "I'd better go before somebody gets hurt, sorry." She goes back in and closes the door.

"Well, that went well."

"Um!"

"How about next door?"

"Okay, Tom, go for it."

After about three rings, we hear the lock click, and a young man opens the door. He has a Mohawk that swoops down in front with a thin pink stripe running right to the end of it, and it is long enough that he has to keep flicking his head to the side to swing this hunk of hair out of his eyes. He has an eyebrow ring, about sixteen earrings in one ear, and a pierced tongue. We evidently have woken him, and I'm guessing it was a rough night. Rubbing his eyes, he looks a little annoyed at me, but when he spies Hatch, he wakes up with a jolt.

"I'm Malory Winston from the *Baltimore Star*, and this is Tom Williams," I say with a smile.

"We'd like to ask you a few questions about the murder of Attorney Richard Mallor right next door. Would you speak with us a little while about that?"

He never looks at me again. His eyes are glued to Hatch, and he has a big smile on his face and says, "Well, hi there," to him and is checking him out top to bottom.

Hatch takes two steps back and says nothing. He is definitely used to women coming on to him, but guys, I'm not so sure. I do all of the talking, but he never once makes eye contact with me.

"Have you heard anything from either neighbors or friends about this murder?"

"Um, no," he says, still staring at Hatch. Now he reaches up to the top of the doorframe and stretches out, flexing his muscles, still looking at Hatch like he is a steak dinner.

Hatch has had enough. He reaches over, puts his hand through my hair and on my neck, pulls me closer to him, and says quietly, almost in my ear, "Sweetheart, we should go now, we have things to do."

I look up at him and am swallowed up in those brown eyes. "We do?" I ask, and he gives me that little smile of his. Oh how I wish it were true! I can feel a small flame start, and I pull myself together and my eyes away from him. That is the only way I can control it. Man! Those eyes are magnetic! "Oh! Yes! We do!" I say louder. "Thanks for your time," I say to Pinky.

"Anytime you want a change, come back," he says again, staring at Hatch, and Hatch puts his hand on my back and steers me out the door, saying nothing.

"Well now, Sweetie, he really liked you, you devil you!" I say once out on the street.

"Yuck!"

"You never even shook his hand!"

"Well, yeah, God knows where it's been!"

I lay my head back and just laugh out loud. "Wait till I tell Pali!" I say with a smile and hit his arm.

"Don't do that."

"I might have to."

"I'll buy you coffee," he says quietly again.

"Hum, tempting. I'll think on that one," I say and keep on walking.

"Now what?"

"Let's try the Laundromat."

We hurry across the street. I really don't know why because there isn't much traffic. Once inside, we spot five or six people diligently working on their laundry, so we saunter up to that area and start questioning them.

"Could we ask you folks a few questions about the recent murder of Attorney Richard Mallor right there across the street?" I say, pointing.

An older lady standing closest to us says she didn't know him at all or anything about a murder. A young guy a couple of machines down says he didn't know any attorneys. Shuffling down through the crowd, I start to speak with a young woman dumping an enormous amount of detergent into the machine. I raise my hand and start to say, "Isn't that a lot of detergent?" when she turns to face me and I change my mind. She has about forty-eight tattoos up and down her body. Big skulls and a spider web on both sides of her neck. She scares me even before I speak with her so I just smile. She smiles back and extends her hand to shake mine and Hatch's.

"What can I help you with regarding Richard Mallor?" she says so pleasantly. She has perfect diction and a richly toned voice. You can't judge a book by its cover.

"Did you know him?" asks Hatch.

She swings around and starts to fold clothes on a table set up for that purpose behind her. She has an easy way of speaking and a laid-back manner, and the more I look her over, she is not the young woman I thought she was at first. She is probably fifty plus or minus, but still has a very thin and muscular figure. Her hair is very long and deeply conditioned, really rather well taken care of.

"I did know him," she says with a smile. "Worked for him for a while."

The desk for no one!

"How long ago was that?"

"Four, maybe five years ago. I've lost count. He's a complex man, so I moved on." Her smile remains. "It could have been great, you know, but he just couldn't get over Emma Lou, his wife, so we didn't make it, but not for the lack of trying on my part. He's or he *was* a really special person," she ends.

"I hate to bring up old feelings here. We're just trying to get a lead, but nobody seems to know anything at all nor do any of them really know anything about his life, outside of his practice."

"He was a very private person."

"I didn't get your name," says Hatch, pencil poised on tablet.

"That's okay," she says quietly. "We'll just leave it like that," and she smiles at both of us and starts to fold clothes again. It appears she'd been hurt deeply, and her scars are clearly on the surface still. Leaving her alone is the best thing right now.

I touch her arm and say, "Thanks for your time," and then we leave.

"Sad what people do to each other," says Hatch once outside.

I just nod my head yes. "Let's call it a day. I'll start at the courthouse on Monday and let you know what I find out."

"We didn't accomplish much today."

"No, but maybe the courthouse thing will give us something."

"You okay, Babs?"

"Yeah, just, you know."

"Yep."

And we drive back to Oxford.

Chapter Eight

The Burger Shack is one mile out of town and ten minutes from the township office where the zoning board meets monthly. It has been a regular stop-off spot after the meetings for all of the members for some time. Even Richard Mallor used to go and chat awhile after the meetings.

"I miss Rich," says Norman Comer.

"Me, too," states Herb Gottchall.

"He always added balance to the meetings, and he knew a lot of stuff."

"Well, he was a lawyer and should know lots of stuff."

"Beyond that legal crap, he just leveled us out and brought up all sides of things, you know?" says Harvey Mellinger.

"Yeah, he was good."

"You didn't like him, Chuck, and fought him tooth and nail about this deal," says Harvey.

"Well, I was against that one, but we worked okay together in the past."

"Yeah, I guess so."

"I need to scoot. Mary's going to her mom's for a few days, and I told her I'd help her get ready." Harvey takes his dinner check and heads to the cashier.

All of the members had decided long ago to meet the first Monday of each month right after work and then go to the Burger

Shack for a sandwich afterwards. This is a routine they all seem to like and keep.

Herb stands up, too. "I need to get going, too. I'm dragging bottom tonight. I'll see you around." And he leaves, also.

"What do you think about all of this, Norman?" asks Chuck.

"I can't believe he was killed! Right here in North East. It's like something out of a movie, you know?"

"Yeah."

"He must have had a disgruntled client."

"You think you'd change your mind on that extra thirty-five acres for the development?"

"Man, I don't know. Rich was passionate about that tract. I don't really know why. There are lots of them, like you pointed out."

"Yeah, and this area could use that mall. We don't have much here. It's bound to improve the area!" says Chuck.

"How so?"

"Well, jobs for one, it'll make for some jobs in all of the stores and the bank, too. They'd have to hire more people to fill those positions."

"No, they'll bring in those bankers from someplace else."

"No, I mean entry-level people. And how about those fast food places? Those will bring in about twenty or so jobs, and it will only grow, Norm!"

"You're probably right. Maybe we should approve it. It really can't hurt, and those birds can fly downstream a little ways to another area and survive there just as well probably."

"I really think so, too. I'm glad you see it my way. You want another soda or something? Dessert maybe?"

"No, I better get moving. Got an early day tomorrow. See you around." And Norman leaves with a wave.

Chuck just sits there alone for a few minutes with a smile on his face. "Scotty, I think we're in luck. Norman seems to be swaying in our direction."

"That's a good thing, Chuck, a real good thing."

Chuck closes his cell and takes the first real deep breath in quite a while.

Chapter Nine

Lying in bed until 7:30 a.m. or eight o'clock is a gift straight from heaven! I've never done this, not even on a weekend. It must be a sign of getting older, and I can't have that; I'm too young! I jump out of bed, make it up, run to the kitchen, put on a pot of coffee, and jump in the shower. I put on some semi-work clothes—black slacks, white silk blouse, jacket with scarf, baby doll flats—and I am ready to face the folks at the Cecil County Courthouse. I even have a little tablet to compile information on. I look official. I'm not sure what capacity I'm filling, but at least I look like I have an official reason to be there. I lay out a pack of beef cubes and rolls I have in the freezer and will whip up vegetables soup when I get home. I have all of the necessary veggies in the freezer. I check for onions, celery, and carrots, Emeril's meriqua, and a head of cabbage. I am set!

My nails look like crap, so I quickly do some work with an emery board, close enough, and slap on some clear Sally Hansen. I stand there, waving my arms to dry my nails, looking like I might take flight any minute, but decide I really don't have time. I carefully grab my bag and make my way out the door, touching two nails en route.

"Damn!" I say, looking at the damage and negotiating the door lock, when I see my new landlady sitting on the porch wrapped in one of the blankets I put there and enjoying a passage of her Bible. *Oh my, there goes my second apartment!*

"Oh, hi Mrs. Smith. Sorry I was swearing. I just messed up two nails getting out of the door," I say with a smile, like that was a valid excuse.

"Don't you just hate that? That stuff is so expensive!"

"It is, but I'm heading to the courthouse today for the finance company, and I want to make a nice impression."

"Oh, you always look nice, Annie. Have a blessed day!"

"Thanks, you do the same." *Whew!* That went well. She didn't ask me to get out or anything. I throw my handbag and tablet in the front seat and start up the car. Another nice day and I have today and tomorrow off work! Wow, I don't know how to act.

I park my car along the side of the courthouse and go in the front door. There are side entrances, but they all lead you up front to security, anyway. I put my bag through the scanner, show the guard my driver's license, and make my way down to the Recorder of Deeds Office. A young man is at the desk, and I say, "Recent land transfers?"

"Large ledgers to the right, listed alphabetically with book and page numbers listed. Book and page volumes to the left on a rack listed alphabetically with book number first. Need help, ask," he said all rhythmically, like he has done it often. He never looks at me once.

"Those files aren't online yet, so the ledgers are the only source," he adds at the end.

"Thanks," I respond. I have gotten all dressed up to look official, thinking I'd have to verify why I was there. I had my business card at the ready in case, and I could have come down here in my jammies. *I'll keep that in mind for the future.*

I wrestle said ledgers, which must have weighed thirty pounds or so. Scoot over to the book and page volumes and start my search. The name was Jonas P. Stoltzfus with an address of 217 Sunnyside Lane, North East Windsor Township. That must be it, because Windsor Township is what Stan had mentioned when Hatch and I were in the shoe shop. I grab my handbag off the floor, throw my tablet in it, and I am done for the day!

Now I have to go back through town on my way home, and that darn bakery is calling to me really loudly, but I stay strong and drive past it. I, however, do notice a sign in Mr. Mallor's office window that reads office for rent. That didn't take long. How quickly we are all forgotten, and it's only been a few days.

I need gas, so I swing into the Sunoco Station on Main Street and fill it up, hoping all the while there is enough in my account to cover the cost. The machine says okay, so I smile and put the nozzle back in place. Today is payday, being the fifteenth. We get paid the fifteenth and thirtieth of each month, and I have direct deposit, and life is good. I have veggie soup for a few days, unless Hatch comes over, and chicken and ground turkey in the freezer. Lots of frozen veggies I picked up for a dollar per pack, plus I had coupons, so got a couple free. It helps to plan and cut coupons. I put the car in gear and start to pull out of the gas station when two cars hit each other about five or six cars ahead of me on Main Street. Oh, brother! Just a fender bender, but that will tie up the town for a while. I back up and look for another exit. Behind the station, I exit onto Pearl Street and turn left to parallel Main and find my way back the only way I know.

This is residential and commercial—just a few store fronts and an auto dealership. I stop at a stop sign, and on the corner is Howell's Printing Company. In the window are several designs, one of which is the exact snake design I saw on the black jacket worn by the long-haired guy I remembered! I am positive of it immediately and park my car along the street at a meter. I slam a quarter into the meter and make my way across the street.

"Hi. I was just leaving town when I noticed that snake design in the front window. Can you tell me anything about it?"

The guy has long hair, too, but is neat and clean. "It's a snake," he says.

"Well, I can see that, but does it have some significance?"

"No."

"Okay, I'm sure I saw that exact design on a black jacket about a week ago over on Main Street."

"Yeah."

Oh my! "Does maybe a local club or organization use it on their coats?"

"The Band."

"What band?"

"The Band."

"What's their name?"

"The Band."

He is making me dizzy with this back and forth thing with the band! I put my hand on my forehead hoping I can make some sense here.

"You okay?"

"Yeah, I'm good. So let me get this straight. There's a local band named The Band, and they have black jackets with that snake design on the back. Am I right so far?"

"Yeah."

"Where do they play on a regular basis?" I ask, feeling like Dr. Watson the dentist probably did on occasion.

"Over at Hanks."

"Is Hanks a bar here in North East?"

"Yeah, why?"

"Well, I saw that jacket on a guy, and I was curious about it. It's nice."

"I could have one made for you."

"Well no, I don't really want one. I don't play in The Band. I was just curious about the jacket, you know?"

"No."

I am getting dizzy again. "Well, thanks for your help on that," I say patiently and wave as I exit quickly. Man, I am cooking with gas today!

I call the office on the blind line that goes directly to Cecil County. It's a non-published line that we use when doing collection calls, and it bypasses the front office. Hoping beyond all hope that Pali doesn't answer, I call the number. Pali answers and I hang up. I wait a few minutes and call again, Pali answers again, and I hang up again. *Damn! He never answers when I'm there!* One more try and Hatch answers with a severe attitude. "Hello!"

"It's me, don't let on like it is."

"Well, how do I know it's you?"

"You know my voice. Come on, Hatch."

"Okay, why are you calling on the blind line?"

"Where's Pali?"

"He left the back office, two hang-ups in a row, and he got irritated."

"That was me."

"No kidding!"

"Okay, listen, come to my place after work. I have lots of stuff."

"Stuff as in food?"

"No . . . well, yes, I have food. We'll have dinner." *Good God! There goes my weekly food stash.* "But I have the courthouse stuff and a good lead on the snake jacket."

"Really! Okay, got to go, here comes Pali," he says and hangs up.

"Was that Annie?" Pali asks. "I called her apartment and there was no answer."

"Maybe she was asleep."

"Or maybe she's out running around, possibly trying to get some information on who killed Rich Mallor?"

"The police have that under control, I'm sure."

"You two cannot get involved in this again, Hatch. Somebody is going to get killed."

"Man, look at all those loan applications. I'd better get busy. Time really slips away, doesn't it?" Hatch says with a laugh and huge smile.

"I mean it, Hatch."

"Yes, sir," he says, giving a little salute.

Pali mumbles something about having a real bad feeling about this and goes on about his business. It's that instinct from hell!

Back in my car, I remember that I didn't ask the guy in the print ship where Hanks is, and I have no clue. I just don't have the strength to go another round with him, so I pull out into traffic, hoping to find another spot to stop and ask that question. I drive a couple of miles down the road and there is a Wawa just ahead on the corner. *Who knew! Coffee and directions . . . what more could a girl ask for?*

I pull in on two wheels and run to the door. After entering, I survey the crowd, looking for someone to approach regarding Hanks Bar. All I see are four guys, talking and drinking coffee, and all looking like Larry the cable guy. Kind of heavy, jeans hanging loose, and sleeveless plaid shirts . . . what a foursome.

They all look at me as I enter. I smile and make my way back to the coffee station, still searching for someone I think might be of help.

Lots of young moms with baseball caps on, some have kids with them, some just there for coffee or a latte. An older lady with blue hair and an old guy cleaning the floor. The only one left is a young guy at the register.

"Is that all you need today?" he asks as I put my coffee down.

"That's it and maybe some directions?" I answer.

"Sure, where are you trying to go?"

"Hanks Bar. Do you know where it is?"

He stops what he is doing, and with a broad smile, says, "I'm a regular!"

"Really!"

"Yeah, it's great and so is The Band!"

"Oh yes, The Band. That's why I'm interested. I hear they are great," I say a little less enthusiastically than him.

"You'll love them. They can really play some tunes. You like to dance? I love to dance!" he says and runs around the counter and grabs me to do a couple swirls around the store. He catches me a little off guard.

"Uh, okay, how much coffee have you had this morning?" I ask with a little laugh.

"Lot's! It's free to the employees, and I love it!" he states, still dancing up a storm.

"Go Bobby!" yells one of the cable guys.

The dance continues until I finally yell, "Stop!" He stops instantly in his tracks.

"Well, why are you asking about Hanks if you're not a dancer?" he asks, somewhat perplexed.

"Well, I dance, but not usually in a Wawa!"

"Oh, come on. How about another little spin?"

"No, no, I'm out on business and must get back. I just stopped for coffee and directions."

"Well, okay," he says, walking back behind the register. "Well, Hanks place is over on Sunset, three streets over on the end. You can't miss it."

"So, I could go to the stop sign here on Pearl Street and then turn left and go three streets over?"

"Yup, you'll come straight to it, and they play this weekend. You'll love it! There's a cover charge of five bucks to keep the riffraff out," he says, giving a nod towards Larry and the boys. "So, be aware of that. But the drinks aren't real high or anything and the food's good. I'll introduce you to The Band if you like. I'll be there around eight or nine o'clock."

"I'd like that. I'll be there with my boyfriend, so maybe we'll see you there. What was your name again?"

"Bobby, Bobby Mahan." The name rings a bell.

"Oh, are you related to Charlie Mahan who owns the auto body shop?"

"Yeah, he's my uncle. Do you know him?"

"No, just of him, with the body shop and all, and I guess he sits on the zoning board, too, doesn't he?"

"Oh, yeah, he gets into all kinds of stuff. Real busy guy. Come around eight or nine. I'll have several of my girlfriends with me, and we'll link up and do some dancing like we did today," he finishes with a laugh.

"Okay, maybe I'll see you there," I say and leave.

Real enthusiastic guy, I think while getting back into my car. I follow his directions and come right to it. *Nice looking place and lots of parking. I'll have to see if Hatch dances, AND we'll get introduced to The Band, even better. Hatch will be so pleased with me.*

I park my car right out front of my apartment and make my way in. I change clothes and take my usual run. When I return, it is 12:30 p.m. and time to start the soup. I brown the meat real good, throw in the onions, celery, and carrots, and let them all brown together as well. When the onions look transparent, I throw in two cans of stewed tomatoes and the cabbage, put the lid on, lower the fire, and hit the shower.

When I come out, it is starting to smell like soup. The rolls are thawing nicely, so I need to focus on some kind of dessert. Something light, my soup is very hearty and with the rolls, we won't need much, but I know Hatch lives for dessert, so I have to come up with something. I have chocolate chips, so I make half a batch of cookies, saving the rest for another time and half a batch will be more than enough, I think.

I clean up a little, move the dust around on the tables, and clean the bathroom. It has been so nice all day I have had all of the windows open, and it all seems so fresh.

Hatch knocks on the door about 5:20 p.m., and as I walk to open it, I notice he has his iPod plugged into his ears and is doing some kind of a two-step or something or quite possibly there is a fire on the porch and he is trying to put it out . . . the steps are similar. *Oh, my! And I was going to suggest going to Hanks and dancing this weekend. Hum.*

"Hey, Babs, what's cooking? I smelled it as soon as I got out of the car?"

"Soup," I say.

"And rolls and cookies!" he finishes, smiling while heading to the stove. The rolls are on a cake tin just out of the oven and the cookies are on a plate next to them, and he is a happy guy.

"What's new at work?" I dish up the soup and put the rolls in a basket while Hatch takes off his jacket, tie, and unbuttons his top two shirt buttons and cuffs. I turn around and smile, thinking just how domestic this all seems and how I love it all, possibly too much. He probably has a girlfriend or, like Bobby Mahan, girlfriends, and I surely don't measure up to them. They probably look like Victoria Secret Models and I look like . . . well fourteen or so.

He catches my melancholy and stops in his tracks. "What?" he says just above a whisper and looks right at me. Now he does that picking up on a change real easily. Probably Pali's instinct from hell rubbing off, but I love when he does that.

"Nothing, I'm glad you're here for dinner. I hate to eat alone."

"Well, hate is a pretty strong word for dinner, little girl!" he adds, and we both laugh.

I have to stop doing this stuff. He'll think I'm falling in love with him . . . *well hello!*

"You okay, Babs? I'll bet you didn't rest or have any down time at all today, did you?"

"Yeah, I did, and I'm good and wait until I tell you the rest, but let's eat first."

"Okay. Is that sweet tea?"

I just smile and pass him the pitcher.

Chapter Ten

Frank Sallman pulls up to the Mahan Body Shop and surveys his surroundings. *This must be the right place*, he thinks. He has the name, but not the exact address. All he has is Marsh Street, outside of North East. He walks into the office area and looks around. Nobody at the desk, nor any place else in sight. He is checking out the licensing on the wall when a middle-aged lady comes in from a side door.

"I'm sorry, I didn't hear you come in. What's the name, I'll check to see if your car is ready," she says.

"I don't have a car here. I'd like to see Charles Mahan."

"Oh, sure. He's in his office. I'll see if he's free to see you." And with that, she buzzes an extension. "What's your name?"

"Frank Sallman."

"There's a Frank Sallman here to see you, Mr. Mahan. He doesn't have a car being repaired here. Are you from an insurance company?" she calls to Frank.

"No."

"He's not from an insurance company, either," she tells Charles and smiles at Frank.

"Okay, Gladys, show him back," he says and hangs up.

"Come right this way, Mr. Sallman. Mr. Mahan will see you now," Gladys says with a smile.

She reminds Frank of Archie Bunker's wife, and he wonders if she is as scatterbrained as she was on the show.

Chuck comes around the desk and shakes hands with the young man entering his office. He has long blonde hair and a black leather jacket on, and he wonders why he is there if he has no car being worked on. He can see right away that he is not from an insurance company like Gladys said and guesses he isn't any kind of salesman either by his overall appearance.

"Chuck Mahan," he says, extending his hand

"Frank Sallman." They shake hands.

"Have a seat," Chuck says, now guessing he is a body man looking for work. "Are you looking for a job? Do you do body work?"

"Well, you could say that kind of indirectly," he responds.

Now Chuck is confused and a little annoyed as he doesn't have time for this cat and mouse game. "Just what can I do for you, Frank?" he asks.

"It's not what you can do for me, but what I've already done for you," Frank replies.

"You did something for me?"

"Yeah, as in one Richard Mallor just last week," he says with a smile.

"I don't know what you're talking about," Chuck says and sits back in his chair. Now his heart is pounding and he feels real uneasy about this guy.

"I did a job for a guy named Eddie that I think you know and was promised a certain figure for my services, but to date I haven't been paid and I don't do anything other than COD and that doesn't stand for cash on delivery, but cash on death," and he smiles again.

This guy is an ass and Chuck doesn't know what to say to him or how to handle this issue. "You have a lot of nerve coming here to my office saying this stuff!" he says quietly but strongly.

"You'd rather I come to your home?"

Chuck stands up. "I didn't hire you. Ed did. You have to deal with him, and I don't know what you're talking about here!"

"Really, I can't believe you just said that, when Eddie gave me the complete and total story." Frank is still seated and seems to be completely at ease with this conversation. "You might want to call Eddie now and we'll all discuss this together, since I'm here for my fee."

"I don't even know Eddie. He's a friend of a friend."

"Then call that friend and tell him to get his ass over here right now, so we can settle this thing and be done with it!"

A few seconds pass with them just staring at each other. *This guy can't be more than twenty-five or thirty*, thinks Chuck, *just a kid, a determined one, but just a kid with his long blonde hair and black leather jacket. Probably a motorcycle gang type.* His eyes are dark brown and severely unwavering. Chuck picks up the phone and calls Scotty. Three rings and no answer, voice mail kicks on.

"He's not answering his phone," says Chuck and hangs up.

"We'll wait. You can try again."

Still that unwavering stare. Ruthless is probably the word he is looking for. Chuck dials again, still no answer, but he leaves a message to call him ASAP. They both just sit there, and all Chuck can hear is the clock ticking on the wall.

Chapter Eleven

"How about coffee? And I made cookies."

"I saw them, and, yes, I'll have both," he says with a laugh. He grabs his dish and mine and heads to the sink. "Why don't we take it to the porch? There doesn't seem to be anybody out there right now."

"Oh, I'd love that." I always would rather be outside than in. We sit on the wicker chairs out front and drink coffee, eat cookies, and savor the spring evening. A breeze is blowing his hair just a little. I look at him and pull a small blanket around my legs, as it is cooling down.

"You okay, Babs? Want another blanket?" he asks and reaches over to get a small one next to him.

Now those beer-bottle-brown eyes are on mine, and I say, "No . . . I mean, yes. I'm okay." Those eyes start to twinkle, and a small smile appears on his lips and my flame is back! I think he knows he unnerves me sometimes. He probably even knows about the flame!

"We could go inside and get under a blanket if you want to," he says quietly.

It's that quiet voice that gets me, and that stare is getting rather intense. I know I looked at his lips. What I wouldn't give to jump him right here on the porch and mess up that hair a little.

"A blanket, inside?" I ask slowly like a space cadet. All I can think of is his arms around me and just how good that would feel.

"And you can tell me all about your day at the courthouse."

"Courthouse?" I am now in a confused state and probably look like the dental receptionist in her state of trance.

"You know, the Cecil County Courthouse, and then about your visit to the shop where the jacket was, like you briefly mentioned at dinner?" He's toying with me and he knows I'm falling apart here. And he still has that smile on his face to boot.

A cool breeze hits my face, and thankfully I come to my senses! "The courthouse!" I say with great revelation. "Yes! I was successful there and with the guy at the sign shop as well."

"Tell me about that," he says quietly again, still with the smile!

"Okay!" I throw the blanket off as I am now having what really seems like a hot flash. "The courthouse!"

"Yes." His eyes are still twinkling.

"Okay, well, I went to the courthouse. I got all dressed up thinking I would have to substantiate just why I was there. I had a business card with me and all, you know, and I got past the guy at the front desk who told me those files weren't online yet, so I had to go to the docket books first and get the book and page number and then go to those books, wrestle those babies that must weigh at least thirty pounds, so I had trouble, you know?"

"Okay," he says and takes another sip of coffee

"Then, I wrote it all down, and it's Jonas Stoltzfus's, and I didn't have the exact address, but the property is in Windsor Township, so I figured it had to be the right Stoltzfus, so I wrote down the road name. I mean, how many Stoltzfuses can there be? So I left there and, coming back through town, there was an accident, so I took a side street. Okay, I stopped for gas first, then took that side street, and found the jacket shop, you know with the snake on it."

"Yes."

"The guy there was a real dickhead and wanted to make me a jacket just like it, but I told him no, I don't want a jacket like The Band!"

"What band?"

"The Band. That's the name of the band who wears the jacket with the snake, the exact one I saw on the guy outside the shoe shop, and they play at Hanks almost every weekend according to Bobby Mahan, who I danced with in the Wawa store when I stopped to get directions. I was there after the sign shop and after I called you on the blind line."

"Wait a minute, you danced with some guy at the Wawa store?"

"Well, yeah, Larry and the boys were just sitting there drinking coffee and not looking too bright, and I didn't think that the lady with the blue hair would know about Hanks Bar, so I went to the guy at the register, and he's Chuck Mahan's nephew, you know the guy that Stan told us about who owns the body shop and also sat on the zoning board with Richard Mallor?"

"Okay," he responds slowly.

"So then he tells me he's a regular there, at Hank's Bar, and he'll introduce us to The Band this Saturday night at Hanks, because they play there almost every Saturday night. He said he would be there with some of his girlfriends and I told him we might be there, too." Now I am pointing back and forth between the two of us at that time, so Hatch just nods his head in a *yes* response.

"So, after we danced, I left and found Hanks, and it's real easy to find, so do you want to go there Saturday night and get introduced to The Band?"

"Al righty. Is this decaf coffee?" he asks, lifting his head to look in my cup.

"Yes!" I squint my eyes at him. And to think not twenty minutes ago, I was thinking about jumping him right here on the porch, knowing how annoying he can be.

He just smiles.

Chapter Twelve

Lil is typing up a storm, the phones are ringing off the hook, and Edna is handling customers three at a time at the counter. When all of the customers are gone, Lil says, "I miss Annie."

"Me too! She at least grabs a phone or handles a customer when we're swamped," adds Edna.

"It's like a bus let out or something. Where'd they all come from? And on a Tuesday!"

"I know!"

Pali comes out of a deal room with a loan to type and catches the end of their conversation.

"You know *what*? What did I miss?"

"We were just commenting on how busy we are and on a Tuesday and how much we miss Annie."

"I really like her and her good sense of humor," says Lil.

"Me too," says Edna.

"Yeah, and she has great legs," says Pali.

A short silence.

"Did I say that out loud?" he asks, coming to a complete standstill and looking like a deer in headlights.

"Yes, you did, Pali, but we'll pretend we didn't hear that," Edna comments.

"What's wrong with *my* legs?" asks Lil, now propping one up on her desk and pulling her pant leg up so we all can see. "All the guys think I have great legs," she finishes and turns her leg from one side to the other.

"Jeez, Lil, who hired you?" asks Pali.

"You did."

"It must have been out of complete desperation."

"You love me, and you know it. I'll even type that loan for you. How's that?"

"Well, at least you'll do something today for a change," he says and exits into the back room and closes the door.

"He loves me," says Lil. "I can feel it."

"Shoe polish fumes are making you high, Lil." They both laugh.

"Where were you last night?" Pali snarls at Hatch.

Hatch lifts his head from his loan application and looks Pali straight in the eyes. Pali has that beady stare on him, somewhat like a hawk on prey.

"Why?"

"I just want to know!" he says, a little more intensely.

Hatch ponders telling a lie, but decides against it. "I went to Annie's for dinner, and then we sat on the porch talking for a while."

"Ethel and I drove by, and I saw you."

"Then why did you ask?"

"I needed to hear it from you," he said, still glaring.

"What? We're friends!"

"Do not touch her Hatch! She is *not* to be touched!"

"I'm not! She's a child!"

"She's not a child, she's twenty-something."

"Well, she looks like a child."

"I see how she looks at you, Hatch. Don't let anything materialize here, do you hear me?"

"I do, and it won't, trust me. We are coworkers and friends, that's it!"

"Keep it that way!"

"Loan's ready to close, Pali," says Lil, lifting her pant leg to give him yet another glance at her leg. "I'll wear a skirt tomorrow," she says quietly and leaves.

"What's that supposed to mean?" asks Hatch as Pali walks by.

"Don't ask. She's neurotic," he says as he leaves.

While Pali is closing the loan, Hatch dials Annie's number. No answer. This is her last comp day. Maybe she's gone shopping or something. He looks over at her chair and thinks just how much he misses her. He thinks about Tess, with whom he has been having a hot and heavy romantic fling. Tess works at a local gym as a personal trainer and has been training him in so many ways, for about three months now. Or is he training her? She is a black-haired beauty with long, shapely legs and intoxicating to say the least. She is also moody and can't cook. Their relationship came to a screeching halt last weekend as their differences became more and more pronounced daily. She wasn't what he thought she would be, and, when all of the dust settled, she wasn't fun or understanding or really rational at all. He couldn't really pinpoint it, but basically she wasn't Annie, and he knew deep down that is the real reason. Whether he wants to admit it to himself or not, it is the truth.

Chapter Thirteen

I drive to the North East, Maryland, post office in the rain. When I left Oxford, it was semi-sunny, and I hadn't watched the news or weather. This morning I lay in bed again, and am getting really fond of that. So if it is calling for rain, I don't know it. But I always travel prepared—I always have food, water, umbrella, boots in the trunk, tablets for notes to be taken, charged up phone, sunglasses, cat litter in case there is ice, a flashlight, and my small but trusty shovel for digging out of snow or mud. I learned this all from my dad, who was equally prepared for almost any emergency. When you are out on the road alone, you are on your own.

"I can't tell you where 217 Sunnyside Lane is. Haven't you ever heard of the Privacy Act?"

"Well, yes, I have, but I have this Avon order to deliver, and I have to find my customer."

"Well, I can't do that."

"I used to be able to pay $1.00 through the Freedom of Information Act and get this information," I state testily.

"Well, that act was replaced with the Privacy Act, and we can't do that anymore!" Now he is getting testy.

"I'll pay you $2.00!" I bargain.

He just looks at me.

"My customer is aging as we speak!"

Another look. He isn't going to budge.

"How about I pay you the fee, and you take my picture, and I'll get a passport. You probably have a quota, don't you?"

"No."

"I'm a federal agent in plain clothes, how's that?"

"That can get you jail time."

"I'm leaving now. Thanks for your time." I get a nod. I'll bet if I were blonde with big boobs, he'd have told me, maybe even driven me there.

I get in my car and back out. At the same time, the rural-route delivery man is loading his truck with today's load of mail. I pull alongside him and roll down my passenger-side window.

"Good morning. How would I get to Sunnyside Lane from here?" I ask, flashing him a smile.

He comes over to the car, leans down to the window, and says, "Follow this road out about four, maybe five miles, over a small stone bridge. It's up on top of the next hill. Lots of Amish farms out there."

"Thanks a lot," I tell him and drive away, smiling the entire time.

Once I cross the stone bridge, I start looking for Sunnyside and quickly come upon it to the right. Number 217 is about halfway down the road, and I pull into the lane. It is a long one, as many Amish farms sit back off the road and at once I encounter a major ditch. My car is small and low, and I don't want to get stuck and be at the mercy of Mr. Stoltzfus and his mules to pull me out. I decide I can't take that chance and back up. Today is my last comp day and when will I have the time to come back? I don't want to come out here after work and get caught in the dark. So I pull over in the field, hoping not to get stuck, and the VW drives right on up past the deep gully crevasse area, and heads for the barn. I usually head for the barn rather than the house. The men are always in or around the barn, and they make all of the decisions in their society. The women are usually in the house. I slam my car door a couple of times to bring any dogs around, but see none, which is odd, especially for the Amish, so I get out, open my trunk, put on my boots, and put my heels in the box they just came out of. Again, I slam the trunk closed and watch for dogs, but have no response at all.

I approach the open barn and start to yell for Mr. Stoltzfus as I walk on. Nobody in sight and I hear nothing at all. I walk around the side and immediately hear a low growl. *Uh oh, possibly an old and more than likely deaf dog, but I'll bet he still has some teeth.*

I freeze and see him slowly walking my way. I should put pepper spray in my arsenal of emergency items and learn to carry it with me. He stops, sits down, and I smile, not that I think a dog knows a smile means friendly. He shows his teeth two more times and I start calling Mr. Stoltzfus once again, only louder.

"Mornin'!" I hear from behind me and I twirl around to see a middle-aged Amish guy with lots of pearly white teeth, which is rare, and his are straight and well-taken care of.

"Good morning," I say and reach out to shake his hand.

"That your car?"

"Well, yes it is." *How did he think I got here?*

"Cute little thing, ain't it?"

"Yes, it is and really good on gas."

"Hum," he says.

"I'm Marilyn Winesap from the title transfer office of the Cecil County Courthouse, and I'm here with some questions for our records regarding a land transfer that has recently taken place with a Charles Mahan."

"Oh, yeah, Charlie."

"Yes."

Blank stare from Mr. Stoltzfus. They do that a lot.

"You sold him some property that will adjoin a large tract of land planned for a mall area, is that correct?"

"Yes, thirty-five acres. Was glad to get rid it. It's usually wet, what with all those little creeks flowing around us."

"Okay, and it was just between you and Charles Mahan, nobody else?"

"Nope, just me and Charlie. He paid me dear for it, too."

"That's a good thing for you," I say with a smile. "And the transfer is done?"

"If you mean, do I have the money, yep, I do, and put it all in the bank over at Riverfront."

"Good for you. Well, that's all I really need. Just wanted to confirm that."

"He's a nice man. Has a body shop in town, I hear, and keeps real busy."

"I've heard that. Well, thanks for your time, Mr. Stoltzfus. I'll be going now. Oh, I had to pull my car up in the grass down by the front of the lane because of that washed-out area. I was afraid I'd get stuck in it, but I don't think I left tracks in the field or anything," I state.

"Don't matter. I'm headin' out there to fill some of it in today. Have a load of stone coming here real soon."

"I'll go now then, rather than be in the way of the stone truck. Thanks again."

I don't even change my boots, just get in my car and head out. I hear the dog utter one ruff as I start the engine. As I am leaving the driveway, again cutting through the field, I see the stone truck slowing with his turn signal on. *Man, what a lucky morning.*

So, now Charles Mahan parted with a considerable sum of money already, and that deal is stalling, so he's short and probably not too happy about that one.

I pull off the road, get out, put my shoes back on, and open up my cell. I once again call the blind line and cross my fingers and squeeze my eyes shut, hoping like crazy that Pali doesn't answer again and ignite another cat and mouse game of hanging up and calling back. It might throw him over the edge.

"Hello?" It is Hatch.

"Thank God you answered rather than Pali."

"Who is this? This is a non-published line!"

"Is Pali next to you?"

"Does that mean is he rubbing me the wrong way, or is he physically sitting next to me in the back office?"

Big sigh from me.

"Is that supposed to be heavy breathing, Babs? Because you're going to have to do better than that."

"Will you stop? I'm out here in no-man's land, pulled off the road all by myself, having just dealt with Jonas Stoltzfus, and his dog, I might add, and you're making sexual jokes!"

"Now calm down, Babs. I'm just playing around," he says quietly.

"So, I'm to assume Pali isn't in the office, is that correct?"

"Correct. You're so business-like, Babs."

I can hear the smile in his voice. Partial flame. "Okay, then. Mr. Stoltzfus has already been paid by Charles Mahan and made a beeline to the Riverfront Bank to deposit said payment."

"Okay."

"So, now with this land deal stalling, Charles is holding the bag, with money out, and no real recovery time scheduled."

"True."

"I'm sure he's pissed about that."

"Yes."

"So, what's next?" I ask.

"I have no clue."

"What kind of an investigator are you?" I ask rather testily.

"I'm not. I'm a loan officer and sometimes dynamic newspaper reporter, former census taker."

"I have a headache."

"Go home and think about this. I'll do the same tonight, and we'll put our heads together tomorrow."

"I have to come back to work tomorrow and am getting real used to sleeping in and just running around, and I think I like it."

"All righty then, do you have a rich uncle or anybody who might kick off, leaving you a large cash inheritance?"

"Not even close."

"Here comes Pali. I'll see you in the morning. Bye, Babs," he said and quietly hangs up.

I just stand there with the phone up to my ear and hear the dial tone click on. Sometimes I feel like the loneliest person in the world. I look all around me and see nothing but fields and road. Not another person in sight. I'm really quick prey out here alone, and a chill runs down my back. I have to stop reading so many James Patterson novels. He's great, but scares the pants off me. I slap my cell closed, jump into my buggy, lock the door, and drive down the road towards home.

Chapter Fourteen

"Scotty, glad you called. We need to talk with a Frank Sallman, who's sitting in my office. I'll put you on speaker phone," he said and clicks the speaker button.

"Okay, but I don't know a Frank Sallman."

Frank leans forward and speaks clearly and quietly into the phone speaker. "I'm the one Ed called to do a job for you guys last week at the office of one Richard D. Mallor, Esquire."

A pause.

"Scotty, you there?" asks Chuck.

"Yeah, I'm here. Just what do you want, Mr. Sallman? Ed is the one you need to contact. He's the one who hired you, not Chuck and me."

"You're all in this together, and I haven't been paid yet. Now that I think about it and know a little more about this deal and how much money will change hands, I think a percentage of the take should be my fee, rather than a measly ten thousand for a job so well done. The cops have exactly no leads at all, and it's been over a week. We all need to talk."

"What did you and Ed settle on?" Scotty asks.

"Ten thousand dollars, but I haven't gotten one dollar yet, so the deal has changed."

"Have you spoken with Ed yet?"

"No, I'm talking to you two, and we need to all gather, talk this over, and come to an agreement or news of who is involved here will be leaked to some of our local officials. Now, that wouldn't be real popular, would it?" he says with a smile.

Chuck's heart starts to pound harder, and Scott is completely silent on the phone.

"Did you both hear me?"

Chuck slowly nods his head yes, and Scott says, "Yes, I did."

"You guys all live and work in this area, but I don't and will be moving on soon. I'll be at Hanks Bar over on Sunset Saturday night. I play in a band there. Be there around ten, and we'll talk this over. Bring Ed. All parties must be present. I'll have tons of backup, so don't be crazy and try to outnumber us or get the police involved, because, actually, you guys are just as guilty of this crime as me. Remember, you all hired me, so each of you is an accessory to murder."

The words are chilling, but true. "We'll be there, all of us," says Chuck quietly, and he hears Scott hang up the phone. He pushes the speaker button off. Frank Sallman stands, looks at Chuck a few seconds, and walks out of his office.

Chapter Fifteen

Wednesday morning, 7:00 a.m., and the alarm goes off, making me jump. I hit the button and throw my feet over the edge of the bed. Wow! I have to get back on track. I brush my teeth, don my running shorts and shirt, slam on my sneakers, and head out the door to the cemetery for a half hour run. Not a long run, but hopefully a hard and beneficial one.

I run like something big and hairy is chasing me, wave to the local police car passing, and make my way back to the apartment. I jump into the shower, finish my hair, and slide into my clothes. Being able to walk to work is a treat. Not only do I get lots of fresh air, I don't have to drive and use gas, so it really saves.

Pali is already there, so the door is unlocked. I happily enter and give Pali a huge smile as I walk past the glassed-in back office and head to the coffee area. I hold up a bag as I pass, saying "Breakfast" to him as he looks up. I even get a smile out of him with that. Since I was home early yesterday afternoon, I made a spinach and red-bell-pepper quiche and monkey bread to bring in to treat the staff after my three days' comp time. It has been exhilarating to say the least. I've gotten a lot done on our investigation and had lots of downtime. I read on the porch undisturbed, washed some curtains, and hung them back up. Took a nap yesterday afternoon and basically just fooled around all weekend. It was great and so like a vacation. I'll take another one anytime Pali wants to give me one. I make coffee and put the quiche and monkey bread to heat in the microwave.

Edna is the first one in, and when she smells the monkey bread, she throws her arms around me and says, "I'm so darn glad you're back. We've really missed you! What'd you cook?" she asks and starts peeking under all of the covered dishes.

"What's cooking back here?" asks Pali. "And did you make coffee?"

"Oh, yeah, coffee's done. There's spinach quiche and monkey bread. Help yourself."

"It's green. I don't usually eat anything green," he says, smelling the quiche and looking at me. "Smell's good, though." He has a real suspicious look on his face.

"It tastes like it smells, so try some," I say and hand him a plate.

"Okay, but if I don't like it, I'm not eating it."

Such a child!

"Okay, Pali, you don't have to." It's like working with a bunch of kids.

"What smells so damned good?" Lil asks as she hangs up her jacket and gives me a little hug.

"Spinach quiche that Annie made," Edna says, taking a mouthful and moaning at the goodness of it all.

"It's green," Lil says as Edna hands her a piece.

"Well, yeah, spinach is!"

"What's that? Red bell pepper?"

"Yep, try it. It's really good."

"Okay, but if I don't like it, I'm not eating it."

"Are you and Pali related?"

"I don't think so. He's Italian, and my people are all German," she says seriously.

Edna snickers and Lil says, "What?"

"Pali said the same thing. You're two peas in a pod."

"I don't think so!" says Lil.

"Where's Hatch?"

"He's coming in late. Had to take his car in for inspection."

"Hope he's not too late. This is best when it's just heated."

"What's best when it's just heated, and what do I smell?" Hatch says, pushing his way through people to get to the source.

"Is that that spinach thing with a crust?" he asks smiling.

"You've had it before?" asks Pali. "Annie has never brought it in before."

"No, I had it at Annie's house about a month ago or so, wasn't it?" he asks and looks at me.

"How often are you there?" asks Lil slyly.

Now Hatch thinks about that and decides he shouldn't have said anything. "Not real often, but . . . sometimes," he says hesitantly.

"How's that girlfriend of yours, anyway?" asks Lil. "What was her name? Tess? With all that long black hair? I saw you guys at the movies . . . what . . . about a month ago, when I was with Monty? Wow! What a guy that Monty guy was. Such a flirt."

"Yeah, I remember that. I introduced you to her that night, Lil. I remember. Yes, Tess," says Hatch looking over at me. I choke on my coffee a little because Tess is a complete and total surprise to me. Now, we aren't dating or anything, but the way he flirts, I just kind of thought he might be a *little* interested or something. Just wishful thinking on my part. Disappointment washes over me.

Edna slaps me on the back, and I recover, but can't help looking over at Hatch who is looking intensely at me. *What did I think? That he sits around all the time, like I do? God, he* does *have a girlfriend, and she has long black hair! What a dreamer I am.*

I throw the remainder of my quiche out, get more coffee, and leave the room, stating that I have to get to work. I make my way to the office and my desk where Pali has a stack of collection work ready and waiting for me, and I jump on it immediately. I put Hatch and his long-haired beauty out of my mind and start working at a fever's pace. Busting through calls, I am in catch-up mode and making headway.

"How about lunch?" Lil asks quietly when I stop to dial another number. When I make collection calls, I hold two receivers, one on each shoulder—one for the Pennsylvania line and the other for Maryland. As you end one phone call and note that conversation, you check out the next one to see where it is and what line you'll use. Volume calling takes a while, and doing it this way saves time.

"It's noon already?" I ask, pushing my chair back and hanging up the receiver.

"Yep."

"I'm ready." I look over at Hatch and say, "I'm heading out to lunch, want something?"

"No, I'm good, thanks. I'll go later."

I know by his look that he knows I'm hurt. There is no reason for it, but I am. Lil and I make our way to Pizza Hut, walking all the way to the end of town. It's a nice walk, and it works off some of my frustration.

"Good to be back to work?" asks Lil.

"Yes! I was bored to tears. Spent some time doing some reading and extra stuff, but basically really missed work and you guys, you know?"

"Yeah, we missed you, too."

Settled in, we decide a veggie medium will work and root beer.

"So, what does Tess look like?" I ask.

Lil smiles. "You're sweet on Hatch, aren't you, Annie?"

"Not really sweet, but I could develop a relationship with him, I think."

"He's a good man and not too hard on the eyes, you know?" Lil laughs.

"I'm just not his type, that's all."

"I don't know. Men surprise you sometimes. I mean, look at me—I'm not real attractive and I'm kind of overweight, but men love me because I love them, and I know how to treat a man."

"I need to take a few lessons from you, Lil."

"Well, lesson number one is to be easy going and treat them well, and I don't mean jumping in the sack with them right away. Even with all of my talk, I wait a while on that really. But treat them sweetly, kindly, and with respect. Make them feel they are the only one in the room. Touch them and be open to their closeness. Encourage fun and openness right away. Don't be afraid. If the first one doesn't work out, move on to another, and always respect yourself. You deserve a good relationship or two, maybe at the same time, never hurt you.

Two! I can't even get one going! "Okay, I'll work on that, Lil. Thanks. I'm just too uptight, I guess."

"You're young, Annie, but don't sell yourself short. You have a lot to offer a man, and you'll fill out one of these days."

"Well, if I keep coming to Pizza Hut, I will," I say and laugh.

"Men like a little body to hold onto, you know?"

"I guess. I'll give it some thought and work on that. Um, do you have anything for freckles?"

She just smiles and takes a bite of pizza.

I am full and happy. I suck the last of my root beer down and scoot out of the booth. "Let's do that again sometime, Lil. I enjoyed that," I say, heading to the register. We split the bill and head back in the direction of the office.

"Big plans for the weekend?" she asks.

I just look over at her with a tilt to my head. "Lil, we're talking *me* here, no-life Annie."

I can't say, "Yeah, Hatch and I are going dancing Saturday night at Hanks place in North East, want to come along?" At least that was the plan prior to the Tess information. And disappointment washes over me again. We are such fragile creatures. I was so up and alive this morning and now I could fall into a heap on the sidewalk! I'm pathetic. I need to get pulled together. I refuse to be pathetic. I'll throw it off and act like nothing has changed, but I'm not feeding him dinner any night this week. Let Tess cook! Bitch! I'll bet she can't! Maybe she does things that make up for no food. Oh dear . . . She is not, however, going with us, and if he shows up with Tess in tow, I swear I'll kill her with a paring knife! Wow! That was scary and not like me. I've got to get a grip.

"Okay, Annie? You sure are in deep thought."

Man, she's observant. "I'm good."

"She's not that beautiful. Just tall, long legs and hair, and pretty well built, but not beautiful like a model or anything."

"Well, that helps a lot, Lil! I feel better already. It's not important. Hatch isn't my type, anyway. We are nothing alike really, I mean, look at me, and then look at him. I look like his kid sister or something, not somebody he'd actually date. We're good friends, though, and he has a life of his own. I can't get upset at that, you know?"

She looks over with a smile. "Okay."

"I'm good."

"Uh huh."

We walk back into the office. When we get there, Pali is coming out of the back room, still chewing. "I just dusted off the last of that green thing, Annie. I liked it, even if it was green," he says with a smile.

"I'll write that recipe down, and you can give it to Ethel."

"She won't make that. She doesn't do green, either."

"Really?"

"Yeah, she just sticks to meat, potatoes, and sometimes carrots."

No wonder his coloring is so pasty, and he has to dye his hair! "I'll make it again sometime and bring it in," I say with a smile. "Any of my morning calls show up yet?"

"No."

"I'll dial faster," I say and start again.

Chapter Sixteen

Lifelong happiness is not what usually happens, I've noticed. If there is a short window of fifteen or twenty years, it's a gift. People change, and relationships suffer for it. We stop trying, get lax, and forget to consider the other one first. Annoyances arise and bad feelings are created that harbor resentments. I watched my parents exist in their unhappy, alcoholic state and prayed daily they would change. That change never came. One died and the other continued on as usual, becoming more dependent and needy as each year passed. I am determined to have better.

I am curled up on the couch with a blanket over me and all of the windows are open. I do this. All of the lights are off, and it is dark, but I am too bummed out to turn them on. The fresh spring air is cool and fresh smelling and I am at peace. My cell phone rings. I almost kill myself getting unwrapped from the blanket and to my desk where my handbag and phone are.

"Hello," I say quietly. I don't even look to see the ID number.

"Hey, Babs, it's me."

Uh oh. "Oh! Well, hi."

"Hi, there. Annie, I just wanted to call and tell you that Tess and I aren't together anymore. It didn't last very long, either. She's not the one for me. We just had a short fling of sorts."

"Oh. Okay. I mean . . . I understand. I've had a couple of those myself," I say.

"Okay."

I run my hand through my hair. "I mean . . . no, I haven't. I just lied. I've never had even one fling."

"I know," he says quietly, and I can hear the smile in his voice. "So, are we still good for Saturday night?"

"Yes." And now he can hear the smile in my voice. "I'll put the paring knife away. See you tomorrow."

"Paring knife?"

"Good night, Hatch."

Chapter Seventeen

At 5:00 p.m. on Saturday, I start getting ready for our big outing to Hanks. I am nervous about meeting the guy from The Band, knowing what I know, or at least what I *think* I know. I curl my hair, spray it upside down, and, with that process, gain about two inches of height and fullness. It is all curls and waves, and I think a nice change. Tall black boots with spike heels, a black short skirt, black satin vest top. I'd gotten a dark red, fitted leather-jacket on sale, and I think the combination looks like I am going out on the town. I even put on makeup. Hatch won't even know me. I hardly know myself, but I don't look too bad, if I must say so.

Hatch knocks on the door, and when I open it, we just stare at each other for about a minute.

"Is Annie home?" He looks spellbound, and that is exactly the look I am trying for.

"Let me get my bag," I say cheerfully. "Shall I drive or do you want to?"

"You can drive in those boots?" he asks, now leaning against the doorframe, arms crossed in front of him.

"Oh, yeah, I've worn them before."

"No, you haven't."

"Yeah, I have. I just wasn't with you, and they're a little much for work."

"Huh!"

"So?" I say, looking at him. Now he is looking at my boots again, my legs, skirt, and hair. I really must look different! "Too much?" I ask.

"No, no, not at all. Hanks it is. I'll drive, though, you're liable to poke a hole in the floorboard with those heels."

"This might not be the classiest crowd. We don't want your fancy car keyed or something down past that there Mason Dixon Line, ya know there, fella!" I end with a southern drawl.

"All righty, then."

It is a perfect night, a little crisp, but not cold. Spring is definitely here—my all-time favorite, or at least running parallel with fall. Clear skies, Hatch and I together, and I don't have to kill Tess or anything. Life is good.

We get to Hanks and the parking lot is packed. Two laps through and we have to search for a spot elsewhere. A nearby garage is closed and freed up, so we deposit my little car there and walk back.

"You okay in those killer heels there, Babs?" he asks with a grin.

"Yes, I can dance all night."

"Okay," he says and takes me by the hand and pulls me close, looking over at me with a smile, and I know his eyes are twinkling like I love. "You look nice tonight and very tall."

"I just hope they don't have that damned Dutch beer you and Edgar sampled and guzzled."

"Okay, you want to play . . . I can play, we'll see who gets smashed first."

"Not me. I'm here on business. I never get drunk."

"Uh huh."

We are now at the door, waiting in a pretty long line, and The Band does sound really good. I look back at Hatch and raise my eyebrows at the sound. "Who knew?"

"Not me."

When we get to the desk, I get carded.

"I'll need some ID there, little lady."

"Oh, I'm twenty-two," I say, digging for my license.

"Uh huh."

"It's in here somewhere." I've only brought essentials, a little cash, brush, Kleenex, lipstick, nail file, and a small tooth brush and paste. I've even left my cell at home, knowing Hatch would have his. But I did drop my license in since this has happened before. "There, there it is."

He looks at it, looks over at me, looks over at Hatch, holds it up to the light, and looks back at me. "This better not be fake," he says with a growl.

"I can vouch for her. She's twenty-two," says Hatch with a smile.

"Sure!" he says.

They glare at each other for a moment, and he hands me back my license, stamps my hand, and Hatch's, and we are in.

"Nice guy," I say.

"If you say so."

Now Hatch has his hand on my waist and yells, "I see a table in the corner to the right away from The Band."

It is a surprisingly nice place. Lots of tables surrounding the dance floor and potted palms placed here and there. It is neat and clean, and The Band is deafening! I walk in the direction Hatch is pointing and am surprised to find a small table for two close by a palm in the far right corner. What a find!

We sit, look around, take in the crowd, and try to get our bearings. I don't see Bobby Mahan yet, but he could be on the dance floor, with lots and lots of hot bodies all moving in sync with the beat.

Surely he'll break out soon with that whirling dervish I experienced in the Wawa.

"I'll get you a drink. Chardonnay, Middle Sister?"

"That's good," I say and smile at him. I don't know how he knew that. I must have had some and mentioned it. He retains lots of stuff. I only retain useless information. Hatch is no sooner gone when a big guy with lots of black hair sits down at the table with me.

"Hi, there. I like them boots!"

"Oh, hi. Well, thanks." He looks like an Elvis impersonator with that hair, long sideburns, and a shiny silver suit. He also seems to have shoes that match.

"I go on later, after The Band plays three sets or so."

He is an Elvis impersonator! Good God!

"Got any favorites? I sing 'em all," he states with a huge smile. He has about ten pounds of rings, necklaces, and bracelets on, and I think, *once he hits the stage and the lights hit him, we all might need sunglasses to survive the performance.*

"Oh, I don't know. I guess whatever you decide to sing will be okay," I say vaguely.

"How about 'Jailhouse Rock'!" he asks excitedly.

"Sounds good."

"Maybe I'll see you after?" he says. Hatch returns at that time and stands staring at my new friend. "Oh. Well, maybe not," he says and leaves.

"Don't ask," I say and take a long drink of my wine.

"You can really pick 'em there, ma'am," he says and takes a sip of something brown with ice. The twinkling eyes are back and so is the flame.

"He goes on next and will sing me a song soon."

"Oh, boy. Do you see that Mahan guy yet?"

"No, but it's so packed. We'll be lucky if we even get close to The Band, let alone introduced to the long-haired blonde guy."

Now The Band consists of the long-haired blonde guy who played guitar, two other guys on guitars, one on base who had his nose and both ears pierced with big hoops, a bald guy as lead singer, a bearded dude on drums, and two gals as backup singers. They are really good and I understand the crowd. Now, this place is huge. It has this main floor and a really big bar with the stage adjacent to it, plus there are a couple of tables beyond where we are, separated by some palms and partitions. They look like big tables that can sit eight or ten people, and there are three of them that enjoy this seclusion.

A slow song comes on and Hatch takes me by the hand and says, "Let's dance, Babs, and enjoy the evening, even if we are officially on duty."

"Okay." I hang the small shoulder bag I brought with me on the back of the chair and stand to go to the dance floor.

"Is your bag safe there?"

"Yeah, it only has a few dollars in it and my fake ID," I say, making my way to the dance floor.

"Wait a minute. You have fake ID with you?"

"Well, yeah. I don't want to bring my real license out to a place like this to possibly get stolen."

"How'd you get fake ID?"

"My cousin Ralph makes them on a regular basis. He's real busy, too. It's exactly like my real one, but quite disposable."

"Okay!" he says and pulls me real close to dance. "You know, it's something new every day with you, Babs. You never cease to amaze me," he all but whispers in my ear, and my heart jumps so hard, he has to feel it.

"I think Bobby Mahan is making his way towards us," I say.

Hatch stops and backs up, looking in the direction I am looking, and there he is.

"I thought that was you, Annie, but you look so different," he says, looking me up and down. "Nice boots!"

"I'm Ray Hatcher," Hatch says, extending his hand and giving Bobby Mahan a serious glare, dragging Bobby's eyes away from my boots and to his eyes.

"Oh, yeah. Annie said she'd be with her boyfriend," he says, shaking hands. "And you two want to meet The Band!" he says real enthusiastically.

"Yeah, I'd like that," I say, and we follow Bob through the throng of people. The Band is on break, but Elvis hasn't started to sing yet, so CDs are supplying the dance music. The Band is just hanging out, talking with a few young girls who make me question the guy at the front door, and he taps the blonde dude on the shoulder. He turns around, and Bob tells him we want to meet The Band.

"Frank, this is Annie. She and her friend, Ray, wanted to meet you guys."

"Really, have you been here before?"

"No, but I saw your jacket downtown and thought the design was real cool," I say.

"When was that?"

"Oh, last week or so," I say, but immediately wish I hadn't said anything about seeing him and his jacket at all.

"Where was that?" Now he is looking back and forth between Hatch and me. "I don't remember seeing either of you."

"Okay, well, maybe I'm mistaken, but I'm glad we came here tonight because you guys are really good!" I end with much enthusiasm.

He looks at Hatch and says, "You a cop?"

"No, are you?" Hatch answers, and they glare at each other.

"Well, honey, maybe we should go," I say, taking Hatch by the arm. "Nice meeting you," I say and all but push both of our bodies away from the area.

"I don't like that guy at all," says Hatch.

"I shouldn't have said I saw him and his jacket downtown. I think he thinks I saw him at Mallor's office."

We make our way back to the table, and I guzzle my wine straight down. I need it to calm my nerves. Even my handbag is still there. What a place! We sit and Hatch pulls our table back a little further and scoots another palm over to better conceal us.

"We need to get a lead here, but not get ourselves killed in the meantime," he says.

"I know," I say nervously.

"I think he is highly suspicious of us."

"Yeah."

"Do you want another wine?"

"You bet I do."

"I'll be right back. Don't attract any impersonators while I'm gone," he says and heads to the bar.

"You ain't nothin' but a hound dog!" blares from the microphone.

Elvis is at it on stage, singing up a storm and gyrating to the tune. I don't know what happened to "Jailhouse Rock," but he is definitely working on the dog tune. While Hatch is gone, Frank and three men all take chairs behind one of the screens and are now talking. I can't hear anything because of Elvis, but they are definitely having a serious discussion. No laughter, no loud talk, nothing but quiet mumbling.

Hatch returns with my glass of wine and I hold my finger to my lips to warn him to be quiet and listen. Elvis is outdoing himself, and I can hardly hear myself think, but am hoping he will stop soon. I drink half of my glass of wine in one gulp, eliciting a strange look from Hatch.

"Aren't you having another drink?" I ask.

"No, I need to keep my head about me."

Elvis ends and it must be potty break time as half of the crowd heads to the bathrooms, and now I can hear Frank and the three other men.

"She looks familiar."

"You know her?"

"She seems to know me and my jacket. She said she saw me last week downtown."

"I thought you said nobody was around, and nobody saw you!"

"Look, Chuck, I did a clean job!"

"Yeah, and then come back to squeeze out more money and maybe have an eyewitness! How damned clean is that!"

"She knows nothing!"

"Get rid of her! We can't take the chance."

With that statement, Hatch stiffens and reaches over and takes my hand. I drain my glass and put my handbag on my shoulder like we should leave. Hatch holds up one finger, indicating for me to wait a minute.

"I've got to get back on," Frank says, and we hear the chair scooting back on the floor. "Let me know what you come up with, and I'll get it done," Frank says and leaves.

"This is not good, Chuck."

"I know, Scott, but we'll come up with a plan and cover our tracks."

"I don't like him at all. He makes me nervous."

"We have a whole hell of a lot of money tied up here, and I, for one, will not lose out on this deal. You dragged me into this shit, Chuck, now figure a way out." Another chair scoots on the floor, and I can see a man stand up and make his way from the area.

"Ed, we'll be okay on this, I guarantee it!"

"Just get it done and quickly," he says and walks away. Now Hatch is looking around for a side door, but finds none on this side of the bar.

"We need to leave now!" he says and stands.

"We'll go out the door we came in, but let's wait until the floor crowd gets back to give us a buffer."

The music starts and the floor fills up immediately so we make our way to the door through the gyrating people. Almost to the door, I can't resist a glance back at The Band, and when I look at Frank, he is looking dead straight at us. I turn quickly and run after Hatch who has gotten a little ahead of me.

Once outside, Hatch says, "I should have listened to Pali."

"Why, what did Pali say?"

"He told me NOT, under any circumstances, to try and get a lead on Richard Mallor's killer like we did with Lois. He pointed out how we almost got killed doing it, and I agreed we'd do nothing."

"I think it's a little late now, don't you?"

"Yeah, let's get back to town. I'll drive," says Hatch.

"I'm fine!"

"You had two glasses of wine!"

"I'm fine!" and with that I almost fall off the curb. These heels are cute, but practical they are not!

"See! You're buzzed!"

"I just fell off my heel, that's all, and we're walking at lightning speed here." I put my hand on my heart to prove that I am out of puff. At the car, I hand Hatch the keys. "You're right, I'm buzzed, and it feels great!" I say with a huge smile. "I think life would be better if we all just stayed in a buzzed state!"

"Okay, I'll get you home."

"Let's stop and get coffee like I took you when you had too much Dutch beer. I'm not even close to how you were. I'm not singing any Gospel tunes. I'm not giggling or anything!"

"I wasn't giggling!"

"Oh yes, yes, you were. You were giggling like a little kid." I laugh like crazy at the thought of it all, bend over, and almost fall off of my heels again. These darn things are getting higher by the minute.

We get in the car and are discussing our last adventure when two men, possibly two of the men we overheard talking behind the screen, walk towards their car and notice us. We can tell by their body language that they noticed us—and with interest. They start to walk over to the car and Hatch puts the key into the ignition and starts my car up. Both men run for their vehicle and Hatch guns the car in reverse and says, "Hold on!" My little car moves faster than it has ever moved, and I am impressed it has such pickup. We head out of town going south.

"Why are you going this way?"

"I don't want to lead them to Oxford. I'd like to lose them before we return to town."

Now in my fuzzy state, I think that is just a DANDY idea and tell him so, eliciting yet another stare at me.

"Don't you know? They're right on us!" he says.

I turn around in my seat and see them coming up fast. "Go faster!" I yell.

"I don't think it will! Babs, turn around and hold on!" And with that, he takes a turn at about forty miles an hour. I think we are up on two wheels, and he guns the engine again.

"Did we lose them?"

"No, I'll find another turn."

"Do you know where you're going?"

"No clue." He makes another turn at alarming speed.

I think it best if I just stay quiet, plus all of that fast turning has my head spinning, and I mentally kick myself for having that second glass of wine. I know better. I'm a true lightweight, and I know it, but I was so scared, I thought it might calm me down. Yet another turn, and I am afraid I'll throw up if we go much farther. Lucky for me, we are now on a dirt road and an eventual dead end. Now Hatch tries to turn around, but my car only makes a kind of whining noise. I look over at Hatch, and he looks at me.

"Are we stuck, or has my car died a fast and unnatural death?"

"I think the latter," he says and tries to start it again.

"We can't just sit here and get caught by those two! They scare me!" I say.

"Okay, we'll get out and walk. Maybe there's a little town or something around here, and we can call a cab."

"Call a cab! Where do you think you are? New York City? There aren't any cabs in North East! Especially out here. Where would you even tell them to come and pick us up?"

"Okay, Babs, don't go all postal on me. We'll get out of here, trust me."

"Okay, we'll walk. I love to walk—not usually in killer heels, but I love to walk."

We start up the dead end road on which my car just died and make our way back to the gravel one. We head down the road for about half an hour or so and see absolutely nothing. No houses, no barns, and surely no town. Now I am worried I'll ruin my booths, so I walk as lightly as possible, knowing even this can't be good for them.

Headlights coming down the road. Now maybe we can get a ride. It can't be the two guys who chased us before. They probably followed us into the dead end and found my car dying a slow and sorry death. Hatch starts to walk into the road to stop them, but suddenly discovers it is, in fact, the two who chased us. He grabs me, and we both run into the bushes.

"Hey, you two, come back here!" one of them yells.

A bullet speeds by as I take in a sharp breath. Hatch yanks me around a sharp turn to the right and we keep on running. I hear lots of commotion and grunting behind us, but no more shots are fired. We run for what seems a lifetime, until we finally stop and take a break. We listen, but hear nothing. We are younger and can run much faster than those two guys, but we are not armed, and they are.

Silence, so we rest awhile. We sit looking at each other knowing we made another really big mistake. Another noise and definite footsteps. We need to keep going to get more distance between them and us as it seems they are not giving up yet.

We run some more and stop again. Listening more, but can still hear them coming up behind us. They are not giving up, but neither are we. The ground starts to go downward and we keep up the pace, only to discover it runs into the river.

"Now what!" I whisper.

"Can you swim?"

"Yes, but I don't want to. It's cold, and it's going to ruin my boots!" I say, looking down at them.

"I'll buy you new ones! Come on!"

"No! I don't want to."

"Well, neither do I, but I don't think we have a choice here, Babs, we're out of road and fields."

Another shot and we both plunge into the icy Big Elk River. My breath catches from the overwhelming cold, and I hear Hatch do the same. The water is swift, and we let it take us downstream quickly. Not comfortable, but at least getting some distance from our chasers. We are frozen, but safe.

After what we think is a safe distance, Hatch says, "Let's get onto the bank."

We make our way to the edge where there is a washed-out area and crawl under a ledge of dirt and roots. We listen, mostly to my teeth chattering, but Hatch pulls me close, and I can feel his body heat immediately. There is a full moon and visibility is great. That's good and bad, but at this time, it is good for us. I look up at Hatch and immediately hear men talking above us. They are following the river, still looking for us. If nothing else, they are persistent.

Hatch's foot slips on the rocks, and gravel tumbles down into the water. Directly below our hiding area is a footpath that I hadn't seen before, but now holds Scott and Chuck and one of them has his gun drawn. Hatch grabs a large piece of driftwood and cracks Scott in the face with it at super speed. I scream and grab my mouth, probably trying to shut myself up. But Chuck already has me by the arm and knocks me down. Hatch is still dealing with Scotty, but has knocked his gun to the ground. A vicious fistfight breaks out. I get up and start to run, but Chuck grabs me around the middle of my body, and I can't go anywhere. Once on my feet again, I am close enough to stomp my killer heels into his foot, and he yells out and backs off.

I kick him in the shin just for good measure and quickly run over to where Scotty has dropped his gun when Hatch hit him with the driftwood. I throw it as hard as I can into the river and hope like hell Chuck Mahan isn't armed as well. He is now back on his feet and right on me.

"You dumb bitch! What did you do that for?" he yells and grabs me again.

I slap him with both hands and kick him again. I tear away from him and run back up the footpath, but only get about five feet when he catches my foot, dragging me back down to the water's edge and starts pulling me into the river, probably to drown me. I hear a whack, and his grip loosens. Hatch is at work again with yet another piece of driftwood, and Chuck Mahan crumbles to the ground. I get to my feet and look at Hatch.

"Let's get out of here."

"Good plan."

We head north up the footpath and run as fast as we can back to where we left my car, wheezing and groaning. Maybe it will start miraculously somehow and we'll get home tonight. It takes forever, but we finally find the dead end road and my car. I can't believe it, but can we get it started?

Hatch immediately opens the hood to investigate the area, and I get a flashlight out of my stash in the trunk. We both peer at the engine. I have not a clue what I am looking at and hope Hatch does, but I have my doubts.

"No wires or hoses are loose, maybe it's just flooded."

"How do we unflood it?"

"Try to start it and floor it, in case that's it," he says.

So, I do just that, but when it makes a terrible noise, I quickly let off the gas, not wanting to blow it up. Hatch comes around, ordering me out and gets in to work with it for a while. He coaxes it and coaxes it and finally gets a little start out of it. He works again and finally lots of black smoke comes charging out of the exhaust pipe and I hold my breath, hoping it doesn't blow up. Now, standing still for a few minutes, I realize that every bone and all my muscles are aching, and I am once again frozen to death and, of course, soaking wet. I look closely at Hatch, and he looks worse than I do. Dear God, what a couple!

Chapter Eighteen

"At least you got it running," I breathe while laying my head back against the headrest. "And we can get home!"

"You're going to my place. We'll leave your car at your apartment and take mine. I'm afraid this might act up and stop on us again."

"Okay. I need to get some clean, dry clothes on, though. I'm about to freeze, even with the heat on."

"Okay, but let's go quickly. You can shower at my place. We might have a tail on us, you know?"

"This police work is hard on the body."

"Yeah, that's just why we're going to them right after work on Monday."

"So soon! We hardly have anything to tell them and absolutely no proof that Frank did it!"

"You overheard that conversation at Hanks', didn't you? It seemed pretty clear cut to me that he is a hit man, and you just might be his next target."

"Possibly you're right," I say in defeat.

We lock my car, I grab some clothes and essentials, and throw them into a bag. My boots and lovely red leather jacket are toast, I'm sure. I throw them into the shower to deal with when I get home tomorrow night.

Going to Hatch's place is like visiting a spa. His dad is a judge and his mom is a lawyer in New England and Nana had an antique shop and, by the looks of things, lots and lots of money. Little Ray was the only child of an only child, and he inherited much. The house is one of a kind. I've only been there once before, but I still remember it vividly. All stone and wood, sunken living room with stone fireplace, lots of leather furniture, and russet color carpeting to finish it off. Stone floor entrance and random wood flooring elsewhere. It has a kitchen to die for and several large bedrooms with their own bathrooms. Not real comparable to my place, but we have distinct background differences. We drive in silence. I, however, am not still buzzed—that ice cold river water took care of that one.

"How are your hands?"

"Okay. How is your head, still buzzed?" he asks with a wide smile.

"No, I've found ice-cold river water to be a quick cure for a buzz and will remember that the next time." We laugh.

"We can crash tonight and lick our wounds tomorrow. I'll bring you back tomorrow night, how's that sound?"

"Like a good plan. They know what my car looks like, and that I have a PA license. If they have a way to trace the tag, they'll have my address, too."

"Right, that's what I was thinking about."

"We'll go see the North East police after work on Monday."

"Not officer whatever-his-name-is. He thinks I'm a loony tune now!"

"What's your point?"

"Evans, isn't that it?" I ask.

"I don't remember."

How can he remember lots and lots of stuff, like what kind of wine I like and not remember the chief's name that we have had to deal with on two occasions? Not good occasions, with two dead bodies, but we seem to be frequent flyers with Chief Evans!"

I sink down in the seat and try to ease some of the tension out of my body and, before I know it, Hatch is trying to get me awake. "Annie, we're here." He is speaking quietly, and at first, I think I am dreaming. I jolt awake and look all around.

"We got here fast!"

"You fell asleep just as we left Oxford. It's been a rough night. Let's get cleaned up and maybe some food."

"Okay," I say as I try to crawl out of the car. I am so stiff and glad the car is low to the ground. If I were alone, I swear I'd lower myself to the ground and crawl to the door, but I can't do that with Hatch watching. He all but springs right out, so I stand and walk on weary legs up the wooden steps to the front door.

"Let's get a shower."

I look over at him, head tilted, waiting for another line, but he just points to the guest area I used last time, and I literally drag my bag in that direction. Hatch goes back outside, and I can hear him beating the mud off his clothes. I turn the shower on very hot and just stand there. I wonder if the long-haired Tess has used this shower, and I look around for signs of another person. Nothing, I'd never know. I brought all of my own stuff, though, and now am lathered up, body, hair, everything, and it feels really good.

I partially blow my hair dry and throw on some sweats and socks. The rug on the living room floor looks so inviting and I slither myself out onto it and start some Yoga stretches, knowing this is just what my body requires to get pulled back into shape and lined up again. My back pops and cracks, and I know I am on the mend.

"Uh, what are you doing down there?"

"Getting all my joints back where they were originally."

"Doesn't that hurt? You're all twisted and everything." He is leaning over me and has a pained look on his face.

"No, I love it, and it really helps." I get up feeling much better and make my way to the kitchen. Now Hatch is stretching his back out and rubbing his neck. "I'll show you some moves if you like. It might help with that back and neck, and you could remember them and do them on a regular basis to keep you lined up."

He turns and looks at me with a smile on his face and quietly says, "I'll bet I could show you some moves that you'd never forget, too."

Oh, my! He just can't help himself.

His hair is damp and he smells so good right out of the shower and he has that twinkle in his eye again. I so want to throw myself at him and experience those moves of his, but we both know it cannot be, and so I smile that half smile I use with him sometimes and say quietly, "Maybe someday."

"I'll keep that in mind."

"Okay, hungry?" I continue, trying to busy myself and act nonchalant.

"Very."

I'll cook. We'll eat then rest. It was a big night!"

"Yes, Babs, it was, and we have to stop this before one of us gets really hurt."

"I know. You're right. We'll go talk to Evans and let him finish this up," I say as I nod my head in a yes manner. But I don't say when.

Chapter Nineteen

"What do you mean you lost them?"

"That guy has a really big punch, and he hit me with a hunk of wood. I have a concussion, doc said so!" Scott rubs his head.

"They're real fast and young, so by the time Scott and I got there, I could hardly stand and they still had all this energy, and she broke my toe with those boots of hers!"

"Whatever! At least we got her car, which might slow her down some.

"We torched it! The plates were destroyed, too. We watched."

"Good."

"Where was it?"

"Right there in town. We'll try to find out where she lives and works."

"When, next week? We need this done with, and I don't think Frank intends to stick around these parts real long. As soon as we pay him, he's gone!"

"Who's putting up the money to pay him, and what's with him demanding a percentage of the deal now? What's that all about?"

"I don't know, Ed. You hired him, you figure it out. And you pay him, too! I'm tapped out and so is Scott."

Chapter Twenty

We sit around, drink coffee, and eat everything in sight all Sunday morning and into the afternoon. It is a really mild day, so we are out back on the patio that leads off the daylight basement protected from any wind. The sun feels warm, and I am stretched out in a padded lawn chair with a blanket I pilfered from the closet. I am at peace. The warm sun is removing all the aches and pains from the night before, and life is good. Hatch is asleep in the lounge next to me, full and happy, and I love the contentment of it all. This secluded location is truly this side of paradise, and I decide to just enjoy the moment and take advantage of our friendship and the ability to be here. His phone rings, and he immediately reaches into his pocket to retrieve it. He wasn't asleep, just playing possum!

"Hello? Yeah? When? Who called you? Okay, we'll stop by the house. Thanks," he says and hangs up. He looks at me, and I know it is bad news.

"What?"

"Chief Nelson called Pali to tell him that your car was found torched on a remote road outside of Nottingham. The plates are burned pretty badly, too, but there was enough of an imprint to track them to you."

"Oh jeez! My nice little car? That's two in two years! My insurance company is going to drop me!"

"It seemed to have a slight motor problem, anyway, if that's any consolation."

"Yeah, we killed it!"

"I'll help you get another one."

"That's okay. I know where I can borrow money to get another one. They can just payroll deduct me." We both break out laughing.

"I thought you'd be really upset when I told you."

"I'm getting used to this stuff. Is that bad?"

"No, you're just toughening up, Babs, that's all."

"Yeah, murder and mayhem is normal to me." We laugh again. It isn't really a funny subject, but fatigue does funny things to people.

"So, we're supposed to stop by Pali's when I take you back."

"He knows I'm here with you?"

"He knows he couldn't get you first, and I said we'd stop by, so he knows we're together."

"Okay, should we tell him about last night?"

"He'll freak out on us. You know how jumpy he is. Plus, he told me point blank not to get involved with this murder investigation, and now we are and not doing real well here." We break out in laughter yet again.

I pack all of my stuff and head for the door. I hate to leave this place of tranquil seclusion, but have no choice. We decide we need to tell Pali about our findings. He'll guess anyway, since I have a slight limp and Hatch has a cut on his face and all of his knuckles are raw and bleeding. That *instinct from hell* is probably way ahead of us, anyway.

"Get in here, in the den. I want to talk to both of you." We all sit and look at each other for a few minutes.

"So! What?" Pali, asks, all but leaping to his feet.

"We have a lead on who killed Richard Mallor."

"So do the police!" says Pali.

"They said that?" I ask anxiously.

"Yeah, they're working this case, and you two are probably in the way again!"

"Wait a minute. Who told you they had a lead? Chief Nelson?" Hatch asks.

"Well, nobody told me that, but I'm sure they do."

I look over at Hatch, and he gives me a sideways glance.

"Pali, you can't *assume* because of your instincts from hell, and we need to get this information to Chief Evans soon, so he can get on this, in case they don't have anything."

"It's been, what, five days? Surely they do!" Pali says, throwing his arms up in the air. "They are THE POLICE!" he emphasizes. "You are A LENDER and A COLLECTOR! Look at both of you! You're all messed up! You, Annie, you limp in here and, *you*," he says turning to Hatch, "your face shows me what your mouth won't say! Look at those knuckles! They look like hamburger! How are you going to go into a deal room with those hands and talk with a loan applicant?"

"Wait just a minute, Pali. After I danced with Bobby Mahan in the Wawa, he said he'd introduce us to the guy I remembered with the snake jacket, and we thought we couldn't pass that chance up to get some good substantial information to then present to Chief Evans at the North East Police Department for them to follow up."

"You danced with some guy in a Wawa?" He is looking back and forth between Hatch and me and has a real confused look on his face.

"Yeah, and if we weren't onto something, we wouldn't have been chased and shot at before we had to jump into the Big Elk River!" adds Hatch.

Pali falls back against the back of the couch and just stares at both of us. "Work a half day tomorrow and go down to talk with that Evans guy and tell him the whole story. I don't think I can handle knowing any more of this. Now, go home!" he says and walks out of the room.

Hatch and I make our way out of the house and back to his car.

"That went well!"

"Hum."

"I don't like leaving you at your place. Those guys might put two and two together, since they took your car from right out front here and start snooping around asking questions about you. They'll find you, Babs." He has a concerned look on his face. He is right: we are in a bad place.

"How about I get some work clothes and go back to your place with you. Would that be okay?"

"Yep, at least I'll sleep."

"Yeah, me, too, and sleep is a good thing." Tomorrow promises to be another big day.

Chapter Twenty-one

"If you don't find her, I'll hire someone who can!"

"Look, the cops up there found the car and traced it back to her, so she probably knows we took it and torched it and that we'll come after them."

"Well then, time is of the essence, don't you think?" asks Chuck.

"Now, look, I don't usually do a lot of legwork, Chuck. I'm the one who does the job, remember?"

"I know, Frank, but I can't be wandering around asking questions. I'm a respectable businessman, remember that, too!"

"Yeah, real respectable," Frank says with a laugh.

"Look, you little twerp, I don't have the time or the inclination to waste any more energy on this. You want a percentage of the take, go earn it, and keep my name out of it!" he says and slams down the phone.

Chapter Twenty-two

I grab some clothes and throw them into a bag. Work clothes on a hanger and two pairs of shoes. I look in the fridge and so want to grab some perishables in there, but don't want Hatch to think I am planning to stay a couple of weeks or anything. I don't want to overstay my welcome. I look in the fridge at the leftover soup, barbeque chicken, pickled eggs, and a fruit salad. I baked a pound cake, so I grab that and the fruit salad and stuff them both into a market bag.

"All set?" Hatch asks. He has been in the living room looking through my books and picked out one of my many James Patterson killers, one that scares the pants off me, but that I love, and we are ready.

"You can't beat a good Alex Cross series," he says, holding up the book.

"I know. They scare me to death usually, but they're so good, I can't stop."

"I know."

"I grabbed some snacks for later."

This produces a smile from Hatch, and we head out. We stop, grab a sandwich from Wawa, and, of course, coffee, my treat. We head back out to the patio and consume our take-out, drink coffee, eat cake and fruit salad, and crash back on the lounge chairs. I could get used to this life. All curled up in my blanket once again, I wonder if the long-legged Tess had, in days past, lounged in the same chair I am now stretched out in. I look around it for long black hair.

"What are you looking for?" Hatch asks quietly.

"Nothing really," I say with a smile.

"She's never been here, Annie. I've never brought anyone else here. Just you."

That real quiet voice again and those dark brown eyes. *Oh, my!* I give him that half smile again and close my eyes and snuggle up with my blanket.

Six-thirty and my alarm makes me jump from a dead sleep. I run to the shower, do curly hair again since it brought on such a look the last time. Basic black dress, with black pumps. I look rather professional and all. I'm not sure what kind of a capacity I am trying to fill again, but I don't want Chief Evans to think of me as such a dip stick every time he sees me. I dash out onto the front porch to check the temperature to see if I need an additional coat and find a mild day with a slight breeze blowing that lifts my spirits and the day is off to a good start. I take all of my stuff with me as we head to work in case I can stay at my place rather than infringe on Hatch's privacy again. Although, he really doesn't seem to mind, and I think enjoys my company. We do get along well and have fun, too.

I scramble eggs, make toast, and lots of coffee. We eat, drink all of the coffee, and head out for another day. We are working at a fever's pace again, knowing we only have a half day to clear up a lot of stuff, which only promotes a suspicious look from Pali.

"No!" says Hatch at one point, and I don't even look up.

At 10:00 a.m. or so, Pali comes back into the back office with a question. "Do you want me to go with you down to the North East Police Station and talk to Chief Evans?" Like a dad of truant children.

"No," we both say in unison and keep working.

"Why don't you just go now?"

"You sure?"

"Yes, just go and get back, but I have to know what's happening here. Keep me abreast on this thing," he says. "And tell him all of the facts, don't hold back on anything!"

Okay, Dad!

While he is making that last statement and telling us what to do and what not to do, we are packing the work away, grabbing our stuff, and making our way to the door.

"Where are you two going?" asks Lil, surprised that we are leaving together.

"North East. Be back soon."

"Can I go along? I never get to have any fun."

"That's not how I hear it," Hatch says, squinting his eyes and tilting his head a little to the left as we leave to a chorus of "Good Luck" from Lil and Edna.

I wave through the front window as we pass on our way to the car.

"I'm scared."

"What about?"

"Well, talking to Chief Evans!"

"He'll probably be glad to get the information," he says with a smile and raised eyebrows.

"Oh. yeah, he'll be real glad it's us again," I say, and we speed down the highway.

The North East Police Station sits out of town a couple of miles and is off by itself. It's relatively new with ample parking and a manicured lawn.

"We'd like to see Chief Evans," Hatch says to the receptionist.

"Who are you?" she answers bluntly.

"Ray Hatcher and Annie Barton from Oxford, PA," he supplies.

About that time, Chief Evans is heading down the hallway looking at a clipboard like I've seen the guys on *NCIS* use, and when he looks up and sees us, he stops dead in his tracks. He just looks at us for a few minutes and says, "Not another dead body!"

"Oh no, the same one . . . I mean, we'd like to see you for a few minutes regarding Richard Mallor," I say.

He looks at his watch. "I have about one hour. This needs to be fast."

There is an impatience about him that hints a belief that we are there with questions about his progress and not information that can help him solve the case. *Oh, boy, will he be surprised.* We sit down in the two chairs across from Chief Evans. I look at Hatch, and he looks at me.

"Okay," he starts. "We think we have some information that might help you with your investigation of the murder of Richard Mallor."

"Do you now," he says, leaning back in his chair. He makes a steeple with his two index fingers, holding them to his lips, and starts to rock in his chair, a little smirk on his face.

"We do," I say and start. "One morning, while I was asleep," and I hear him give a little sigh. "Well, I was about half asleep, you know, when you're about half in and half out, you know?"

He just nods his head yes.

"Well, I remembered a guy on the porch outside the side door from the shoe shop, right there at the steps going up to Mr. Mallor's office and the banging of a door. This guy had long blonde hair and wore a jacket with a snake on the back. We tracked the jacket to The Band, a band that plays at Hanks place over on Sunset, and overheard a conversation between him and Chuck Mahan at the body shop."

"Chuck Mahan from the body shop!" he says with alarm.

"Yes..."

"Wait a minute." He gets on his intercom. "Get Adams in here, would you?" He hangs up.

Almost immediately, there is a slight knock on the door and Sgt. Adams walks in.

"You want to see me, boss?"

He looks over at Hatch and me and a look of recognition passes his face.

"You remember Miss Barton and Mr. Hatcher from the finance company in Oxford? They are here regarding the death of Rich Mallor."

"Oh yeah, I remember." He, too, has that look like *oh no, not these two again* on his face.

"Have a seat. These folks have some information that I need you to hear."

"Okay." He settles himself in a chair he pulls up and sits next to the chief.

"Would you start again?" the chief asks. He hands Adams a tablet and pen and gets ready to take down the information himself.

"Sure." I go over exactly what I told the chief before and add the names of the two other men, Scotty and Ed. Hatch fills in the information about Chuck sitting on the zoning board and about the Marshall Deal that he obtained information about through his dad,

Hub, who sits on the Riverfront Bank Board of Directors and the thirty-five acre problem. I see eye contact between the chief and Adams several times.

"We have the information regarding the thirty-five acres Chuck Mahan bought from some Amish man to resell to the developer."

"Jonas Stoltzfus on Sunnyside Lane," I supply, and the chief raises his eyebrows at me, indicating he is just possibly impressed with our investigative work. I sure hope so.

Hatch continues. "Now, it seems Charles Mahan and these two other investors put a lot of money out for the thirty-five acres, but Richard Mallor wouldn't give the nod for approval with the zoning board due to some birds and ducks that were making homes there and Mahan was not happy with that at all."

"How did you hear that?" Adams asks.

"We heard it from Stan at the shoe shop when we went down to talk to him about the guy with the jacket," said Hatch.

"I was talking with Stan before I went up to see Mr. Mallor the day I found him and didn't think a thing about that guy, because I just briefly glanced over at him, and I wanted to see if Stan remembered him, too," I added.

"Did he?"

"No."

"You're sure about this guy?"

"I am positive. Then when I was in North East, at the courthouse trying to get the name of Mr. Stoltzfus so I could go talk with him about the thirty-five acres, I had to take a detour because of an accident and saw that exact jacket in Howell's Print Shop, so I went in, and the guy there told me The Band had those exact jackets."

"What band?" Adams asks.

"The Band!" we all say in unison.

"They play at Hanks."

"Oh, yeah, yeah."

"Keep up here, Adams. You taking this down?"

"Yeah, boss, yeah."

"Then, when I left there and stopped to get coffee and directions to Hank's place, I met Chuck Mahan's nephew, Bobby, who is a regular at Hanks, and while we were dancing, he said he'd introduce us . . ." I point back and forth to Hatch and myself "to the Band Saturday night."

"You danced with some guy in the Wawa?" Adams again.

"Yes, but I don't usually."

"Okay," he says slowly.

Hatch continues. "We went Saturday night and met they guy with the long blonde hair and jacket. He was really evasive, especially with me, asked me if I was a cop. When Annie said she had seen him downtown and noticed his jacket, he looked at her like she was prey. We immediately went back to our table, and after Elvis was done, we heard them talking about getting rid of Annie."

"Elvis?" Adams again. He gets a stare from the chief.

"An impersonator. Not bad," I say.

"How did you hear this? Where were they?"

"There are a couple of tables behind a partition—for some privacy, I guess—at the end of the dance floor, and when The Band was on break he, the blonde guy, whose name is Frank, went over behind the partition and was speaking with the other three guys. One was Chuck Mahan and this Scott guy and an Ed."

"If you go questioning Chuck Mahan, guarantee he has a few cuts and bruises on his head and knuckles like I do, and Scotty has a face full of splinters," Hatch said, and we look at each other with a nod.

Another look between the two officers. "I'm afraid to ask why you are all are beat up."

"Well," I continue. "We left Hanks' and were immediately approached by two men— this Scotty guy and Chuck Mahan—and they chased us. My car stalled, so we got out and walked a while, and they caught up with us, shot at us, and we had to jump into the Big Elk to get away from them."

Hatch continues. "We hid in a wash out along the river bank because we were so cold, hoping they would keep on going, but they approached us with Scott's gun drawn. I hit Scott across the face and head with a good-sized piece of driftwood lying right there, and he went down, dropping his gun, but got right back up, and we had a fistfight that lasted a while. The guy's in pretty good shape."

"In the meantime," I say, "Charles Mahan threw me down on the ground, but didn't have a gun, so when I got free, I ran over, picked up the gun that Scott dropped when Hatch hit him with the driftwood, and threw it into the river. Now that really pissed Mahan off, and he dragged me back to the water and was going to drown me when Hatch hit him over the head with another piece of wood."

They both look amazed with all of this and start writing furiously in their tablets.

"How'd you get away?" Adams asks really excited.

"Once loose, we ran really hard and got back to where my car was, and Hatch got it started."

"It was only flooded and I got it to turn over pretty fast. We left it at Annie's apartment, which is right there on North Third Street in Oxford, and we went to my place for the night."

I continue. "My car was found torched in Nottingham, but there was enough of an imprint left on the license plate to trace it to me. The Oxford Police Department notified our boss, Edward Palizzi, at his home, and Pali contacted Hatch."

They both are just staring at us and say nothing at all.

"What do you think?" asks Hatch quietly.

"It's quite a story!" Evans says with a laugh.

"It's not a story. These are the facts, and we think you need to act on them," I finish.

"Chuck Mahan is a well-known businessman in this area, and I, for one, don't feel he'd ever be involved with something as violent as murder."

"The last thing we heard from the conversation involving these three was 'get rid of her'. And I, for one, don't like the sound of that," Hatch remarks. "She needs police protection, especially at night. She lives alone and is very vulnerable now." He has an intense stare-down going on with Chief Evans.

"We could put a man on that, you know, watch the apartment at night and all."

"I'd feel a lot better if that could be arranged starting tonight."

"Okay, we will, and we'll do some checking around, too." Now he glances at his watch and indicates we have used up our allowable time, so we stand, shake hands with both officers, tell them thanks for their time, and leave.

Back in the car, I look at Hatch and say, "What do you think?"

"He thinks we're both dip sticks," he says and starts his car, a concerned look on his face.

Chapter Twenty-three

I lock the door and make my way to work. I was too exhausted to run earlier, so I stayed in bed later than I should have. A restless night left me tired, and concern is taking its toll on me. I have a corporate customer coming in this morning, so I put on a decent suit with a red jacket and black skirt. I decide to wear red heels, even though I know they will bring on several smart remarks from someone at work, but at this point, I really don't care.

Coffee is first on the agenda, so I make lots of that first and get all of my collection work out of the filing cabinet. Pali is already there when I get to the office, so when I sit down to make calls, the first remark starts.

"Morning, Dorothy! Been to Kansas lately?" With a smile and a sly look.

I just smile and shake my head.

Hatch is out front talking to a woman and finally comes in with a smile.

"Is that a customer?" asks Pali.

"No, I don't think so. She just appeared at my car when I parked and followed me to the office," he says with a smile. "Rather desperate acting though," he says to me as he sits down in his chair. "And, how's Toto? Seen any tornadoes lately?"

"Only you," I respond.

This brings on a Colgate special and he seems real pleased with himself. *Nobody ever follows me to work!*

"I have the name of another attorney we need to talk to in Maryland to send our stuff to," Pali announces.

"When are you meeting with him?" I ask.

"I'm not, but Hatch has an appointment with him in a little over an hour." He also seems pleased with himself.

"Okay, where am I going?"

"I'll write his address down. He knows somebody's coming today. I didn't say who. His name is Eastridge, and I hear he's real good, too, just like Rich was."

"Okay."

We all do our usual thing, mostly on the phone. Hatch asks me if I saw anybody covering the area from the police department last night. I shake my head no.

"Probably plainclothes," he says.

"Right," I respond. Hopefully somebody was watching as I am feeling more concerned as time goes on. I didn't get a strong feeling of concern from the officers at the North East Police Department.

"I better get going," Hatch says, looking at his watch.

"See you later," I say, still dialing.

He pulls a hunk of my hair as he passes by my chair on his way out and leaves for North East.

His empty chair next to me makes me think how much I need his presence to feel comfortable. Being with him at his house all day Sunday was fulfilling, and we never even touched. My heart is doing funny things when it comes to Hatch, and I am probably heading for a heartbreak.

I meet my corporate guy, set new perimeters for him, and make more calls.

"How about lunch?" Lil asks as she sticks her head in my door.

"I need to go home today. I have too many leftovers and don't want to lose them. Want to come, too, and have veggie soup I made?"

"No, thanks. I have a mean taste for a steak sandwich."

"Okay, another time."

Another few calls and I'll go. I call a Mr. Lowell.

"Hi, is this Mr. Lowell?" I ask.

"Yes, it is," he answers.

"Mr. Lowell, I'm trying to reach Lewis," I say. Lewis is the son, and he's not the most reliable person. Mr. Lowell is a small black man about my size and always wears a little hat and very small, wire-rimmed glasses.

"He's not here."

"Do you know what time he's expected, or where I could reach him?"

"No, but I could get you his phone number," he replies.

"Okay."

"I have to lay the phone down and get my glasses," he says.

"Okay, take your time."

I can hear him talking to himself and shuffling around. He comes back to the phone and asks if I can hold on a little longer as he has to raise the shades so he can see, since he hasn't done that yet.

I say, "That's okay, I'll hold."

Once again, he quietly lays the phone down, and I can hear him still mumbling to himself, moving papers, and finally he comes back and says, "Okay, I'm back."

"Okay, thank you."

He clears his throat with much fanfare and says, "Okay, here's his number." And he gives me the number I've just called.

"Well, that's the number I just dialed!" I say.

"Well, yes, he lives here with me!"

That does it! It's time for lunch! Pali is on the phone, screaming at one of his customers, and I just wave and say, "Lunch."

He waves and continues his feverish conversation.

"See you ladies later," I say, walking out and getting a dual response of, "Okay."

I should have brought low-heeled, old shoes to walk back and forth to my apartment, as some of the sidewalks are brick, and I'm sure hard on heels, but I didn't, so I have to walk lightly. I am just two houses from my apartment house when I hear tires squeal, and as I look around to the street to see what is happening, two guys I've never seen before grab me and pull me into the car. I start putting up a fight, and they pick me up and literally throw me in the back seat head first. One gets in back with me and the other jumps in the passenger side of the front and the driver speeds off.

Pali has finished his terroristic phone call and it dawns on him that he is going to be out longer than usual for lunch, so he needs to tell me the follow-up on his irate customer in case he shows up at the office, which sometimes happens.

"Has Annie already gone?"

"She just left," says Edna.

Pali hustles into a little jog, trying to catch me before I am too far down the street. He runs out onto the sidewalk just as I am being thrown into the car, and he sees two men shoving a person in a car, and she has red shoes on.

He is startled, but Pali is never completely rattled and always maintains composure and keeps his head about him. The first three letters of the license plate are HGY and there is a three in there somewhere. It is a Maryland tag, too. He turns around in one circle and runs back into the office repeating the letters and the three to himself.

"Give me a pen!" he yells to Edna as he gets to the counter.

"Well, okay!" she says perturbed.

He writes down the letters and looks at Edna.

"Damn, this is bad! This is really bad!

"What!"

"Really, really bad," he keeps saying as he makes his way back to his office.

Edna just shakes her head.

Lil comes back with two cheese steak sandwiches, one for her and one for Edna, and is a happy girl.

"Pali's cracking up," says Edna.

"What's new? Let's eat." They open up their lunch.

Pali's hands are shaking so badly he can hardly dial Hatch's number.

"Hello?"

"Two guys just snatched Annie off the street as she was going home for lunch and threw her in a car!" Pali yells like Hatch is in Egypt.

Lil has a mouthful of cheese steak, and Edna is just about to start on hers, when they hear Pali, and their eyes fly wide open. They both run to the back office to hear more.

"Shit! What kind of a car was it, Pali, did you see?" Hatch demands.

"Yeah, black sedan, new, and had a Maryland license with H-G-Y and a three, but that's all I remember."

"Call Nelson and I'll come right up."

"No, they're evidently heading somewhere in Maryland! Go to the Wawa there on Route 1, and I'll call Nelson and have him work on that plate and see if he can give us a lead on whose it might be. We'll go from there and get that Evans guy involved, too."

"Okay, hurry up. I'll see you there."

Pali stands up and looks at Lil and Edna, and says, "I have to leave for a while."

"Oh no, you're not going without us!" Edna says.

"Yeah, we can help!" says Lil.

"We can't *all* leave!" Pali remarks.

"We'll put a sign on the door stating there was an emergency and we all had to leave," says Edna, grabbing Pali by the arm. "We can't just let somebody get our Annie!"

"Lil, make a sign, we'll put it on the door!" Edna yells and runs out to wrap her sandwich up and tuck it into her handbag.

"Should I write it or type it?"

"Jesus, Lil! Just wing it and make it fast!"

"Okay, okay, don't holler at me! I hate to be hollered at!"

Pali looks at the two running around the front office, throwing the cash drawer money in the safe, stuffing their sandwiches in their pocketbooks, and making a sign and sticking it on the door. Lil goes back and puts the cover on her adding machine, and he yells, "Let's go!"

They all run like little kids towards the front and out the door. Pali drops his keys twice trying to lock the door, and both women say, "Come on!" They run to Pali's car parked in a little side lot and jump in like Keystone Cops. He backs out at forty miles per hour and the chase is on.

Chapter Twenty-four

I am rubbing the top of my head where it hit the door handle, but at least I'm in a sitting position, as we weave our way through streets at a fast pace, heading for Maryland. I hope like heck that a patrol car is close and we'll be stopped for speeding. I know most of the local police, since I usually see one of them while I'm running in the mornings and wave. The guy in the back seat with me looks a little spaced out, and I am truly afraid. Nobody is saying anything, so I think I'll start. "Where are we going?" I demand.

"Shut up!" says the guy next to me.

"I want to know where we're going!" I say again.

"Give me that bag!" He grabs my handbag, throwing my cell phone out the window. Now looking through my bag and finding nothing of interest, he throws it back at me. That phone was not cheap, which really makes me mad, and I *so* want to kick him in the leg with my red shoes, but I know he'll just punch me in the face or something and I don't want to have to replace teeth. A complete and total fear sweeps over me. When Hatch and I are together, I'm afraid somewhat, but the bottom line is, I know he'll take care of the situation and me as well. Right now, I am on my own. At least I wasn't blindfolded or anything, so I take mental notes of where we are going in case I can get away from them and call Hatch's cell. Chances aren't good, though, because there are three of them and only one of me.

In through North East proper and over several streets. I know at that point we are heading to Mahan's body shop. Now I am worried that since I wasn't blindfolded, they don't care whether I know where we are going because I'm not coming out alive anyway.

Chapter Twenty-five

Pali speeds down Route 1 at eighty miles per hour, heading to the Wawa store, Edna is up front holding firmly onto her handbag with the steak sandwich in it. Lil has hers out, and the car smells like a deli.

"Good God, I'm hungry. What do I smell?" asks Pali.

"Our steak sandwiches," Edna remarks. "But how can we think of food at a time like this?"

"Easily, I didn't have lunch!"

"I'll give you half of mine when we get to the Wawa," Lil answers, her mouth full while she is consuming her half in the back seat.

"I'll save half of mine for Annie. She's probably hungry, too," Edna says nobly.

Pulling into the Wawa on two wheels, Pali recognizes Hatch's car on the side of the parking lot and pulls in next to him.

"Any word from Nelson?" Hatch asks concerned.

Just then, Pali's phone rings, and he flips it open. "Yeah?" he answers. "Okay, I'll find it. Okay, thanks a lot!" he says and closes his phone. "Mahan's Body Shop. That car's registered to them. Where is it?"

Hatch never even answers, but turns and runs inside the store with Pali, Edna, and Lil right behind him.

"Excuse me, how do I get to Mahan's Body Shop?"

"I dunno," says a young girl at the register. "I never heard of it," she says and smiles at Hatch, twisting a hunk of her hair around her finger. When he turns around to look for another person to ask, he sees and recognizes Scotty, who he had the altercation with Saturday night. Scott recognizes him, too, and runs out the side door, with Hatch in hot pursuit.

Pali, Edna, and Lil don't even notice. Pali is ogling the sandwich case, Edna is heading for the coffee station, and Lil is smiling and winking at some trucker holding a bag of chips in the register line.

"Who knows where Mahan's Body Shop is?" Edna all but screams and everybody looks her way.

"I do," says a young man behind the hot sandwich counter.

"Good God, I'm so glad. I need to find my friend, Annie! She's there with a bunch of thugs!" she says excitedly.

"Oh, okay. You go out here, turn right onto Pearl Street and then over two more streets to Marsh. Mahan's is there on the corner of Marsh Street."

"Thank you, bless you, thank you." She runs for the door, calling Pali the entire time.

Lil pulls herself away from the trucker and runs after them. Back in the car, Pali guns it and follows the instructions.

"Can't we go any faster?" yells Lil.

"There are cars in front of me, Lil! How do you expect me to go faster?"

"Go around them, go around!" Lil yells, leaning forward between the front seats and pointing. So Pali drives around, up on a curb, on some lawn to a fabric shop, missing a fire hydrant by a hair.

"Damn, I thought you had that hydrant!" Edna yells.

"Hold on!" yells Pali. He goes around another group of cars and luckily doesn't have to negotiate any large obstacles.

Mahan's is right there on the corner as they were told, and he pulls in on a mean angle and they all run inside.

"Where's Annie?" yells Pali to the lady at the desk.

"Annie who?" she asks, hand on heart and quite breathless.

"Annie Barton! I know you guys have her here. She's been abducted right off the street and I saw it happen!"

"Oh my, when did this all take place?"

"Right around noon, and I need to find her now! Where's Chuck Mahan?"

"He's not here right now, and I don't know where he is!"

Pali runs past the front desk area and into the shop where several guys are working on cars.

"Where's Charles Mahan?" he yells.

"Not here, did you check his office?"

"Dammit, I need to find him and now!"

"I'll look in his office for you. Do you have a car here?" one of the men asks.

"No, I don't have a car here! I just want to talk to Charles Mahan!"

"Okay, fella, I'll check for you," the mechanic says and leaves to go find Mahan, coming back in a minute. "He's not there."

"Oh jeez!" says Pali and leaves the shop area.

"Where's Hatch?" he yells when he gets back to the front office.

"You know, I haven't seen him since we were at Wawa's," says Edna.

"Me neither," says Lil, picking steak out of one tooth.

"I thought he was coming here!" They all stand there looking at each other. Two patrol officers walk in the door and ask for Charles Mahan and the questioning starts all over again.

Chapter Twenty-six

The thought of having to fight his way through another couple of locals doesn't sit well with Hatch, but he will find Annie before the day is over if it kills him.

Scott is three cars ahead of him, but he can still see him. He has to know where Annie is, and he is his only lead. Pali is probably at Mahan's by now and noticing that he is not, so he dials Pali's cell.

"Yeah?" answers Pali.

"It's me. I'm following the guy I beat up Saturday night that I saw in Wawa. He ran out the side door when he saw me, so I'm thinking he's aware of what's happened. Where are you?"

"At Mahan's and he's not here, and even better, nobody knows *where* he is."

"Damn!"

"The North East police are here and are putting an APB out on the car now, but it's been at least an hour and a half. They could be anywhere."

"I'll keep you posted on the guy ahead of me. Call me with any update."

The guy is still driving, but is clearly going in circles, knowing Hatch is behind him. As one can imagine, Scott is not well-prepared for a chase and must run out of gas since he pulls into a station and Hatch is right on him. When Scott pulls into the pumps, Hatch pulls in front of his car, blocking his exit, and with both fists full of Scotty's shirt, slams him into the gas pump.

"Where is she?" he says quietly in his face.

"Where's who?"

"Don't be cute with me, Scotty! Remember the driftwood Saturday night? I'll beat the hell out of you again, I swear I will!"

"I don't know where she is!"

"Yes, you do!"

"No I don't."

"I have a lighter in my pocket, and I'll douse you with gasoline and light your shirt, I swear I will!" Hatch says louder now.

"No! You wouldn't!"

"Try me!"

"I don't know where she is!"

Hatch reaches over and grabs the pump handle, splashing gas on Scott.

"No, no! I'll tell you! Don't do that!"

"Where?"

"There's an old house Frank Sallman has been renting outside of North East, over on Old Possessions Road. He has her there!"

"How do I get there?"

"South on One, to Old Oaks Bridge."

"I don't know Old Oaks Bridge!" He slams him up against the tanks again.

"It's about five miles down this road." He points to Center Street.

"It merges with Route 1. Follow it about three miles, turn right onto Old Oaks Road, over the bridge, and then turn left onto Old Possessions Road. The house is all by itself on the right. It sits back a ways from the road, but you can see it. It's all black pine boards."

"You better be telling me the truth, or I swear to God, I'll find you, Scott, and finish this! Do you understand?"

Scotty just nods his head yes.

Hatch follows the directions and spots the house right away. He drives past it, tucking his car into a grassy area behind some pines. He isn't sure what he will find once he gets to the house, but needs distance to observe the area and make the right decision. Annie's life might depend on it. There is only one truck at the house. No black car like Pali described, and no sign of Annie. He wouldn't be surprised if Frank Sallman is armed—he looks the part, and Hatch has nothing! A good-sized stick with a knot on the end is close by his feet, and he grabs it. It is better than nothing. He watches a while and makes his approach. He circles around behind the house, hoping he can see in the window at least to get an idea of how many people he is up against, but he sees nothing. He starts to approach the house when the black sedan rolls down the road and slides into the driveway. Hatch hits the ground and hides behind several bushes and watches. Annie is in the back seat. Two of the men get out, one dragging Annie with him, and the driver backs out and leaves. So, two guys and probably Frank Sallman inside. Now Annie pitches a fit. She kicks the hell out of the one guy and hits him, trying to get loose. The other guy goes over, grabs her by the arm, and now she is between both men and not able to do a thing. Frank Sallman steps out onto the front porch, and all four go inside.

Hatch's heart jumps a foot. He is no match for three guys, and he knows he needs backup. He shouldn't have come out here alone. About that time, he sees a car coming down the road and knows instantly it's Pali! And he has Edna and Lil with him! Hatch jumps up from his hiding spot in the bushes and waves his arms, pointing down the road to where he left his car.

Good God, what are you all doing out here? he thinks.

He runs over the hill and through the trees until he reaches his car where Pali has pulled in next to it on the grassy area. Pali climbs out of the car, eating a steak sandwich and looking all around. Hatch holds his fingers up to his lips, indicating they need to keep quiet and goes over to them. "How did you find this place?" he whispers.

"Oh jeez, we stood around the body shop for an eternity, waiting for that Mahan guy to show up, but he never did, but that Scotty guy came tearing in, all strung out, had gasoline all over him, yelling for Chuck and saying there was a crazy guy threatening to kill him or set him on fire if he didn't talk. He was just this side of hysterical, and I thought he probably had an encounter with you. He told us how to get here."

Hatch smiles.

"Where's Annie?" Edna asks breathlessly.

"In the house, but Frank Sallman, the guy who killed Mallor, is in there, too, and two of the guys who grabbed her. The black sedan just dropped off her and the two thugs not five minutes before you got here."

Pali finishes his cheese steak and asks Edna if she has anything to drink. They all just look at him, and he shrugs his shoulders.

"We need a plan and fast," Lil says.

"We need to either create a diversion or something to stall their plans," says Edna.

"What, we should blow up something? What with? You watch too many movies!" Pali yells at Edna.

"Don't yell at me! You're the one who sent her down to North East to begin with, and she found Mr. Mallor! it's all your fault!"

Lil says, "Yeah!"

"Let's all settle down here," Hatch says quietly. "We're all arguing here, and they could be beating Annie up as we speak. We need to work together and fast!"

"Okay, okay, I've got it. We'll drive up to the house and pretend we're potential buyers with our real estate agent," and she points to Edna.

"We'll go to the door and create this stall, and Hatch can go around and come in the back door and grab one of the guys. We'll handle the others. We'll take them by surprise!" Lil states all excited.

"I like it!" Edna says.

"I hate it!" says Pali.

"Do you have a better idea?"

"No."

"And we have no time at all here. We need to do this and now!"

"Okay, okay, we'll go in your car, Pali. Wing it from there on," Edna says and crosses herself.

"I didn't know you were Catholic," Lil states while climbing into the car.

"I'm not, but we need all the help we can get."

"Let's be real loud, so they hear us right away."

Hatch runs back through the woods towards the house.

Pali, Edna, and Lil pull into the driveway and all leap out.

"You'll love this place, it's so quaint, and the privacy here is outstanding!" Edna yells.

"Oh, Sweetie, I love privacy. We can do whatever we want to, whenever we want." Lil takes Pali by the arm and kisses him on the cheek.

"What the hell?" Frank says as he looks out the front window.

"Who are they?" yells one of the men.

Now on the porch, Edna just walks right in the house.

"Come right on in. We'll have a good look around. You'll love all of the open beams. I do—oh! Hello!" she says when Frank meets her almost at the door.

"Big Buy Real Estate. I'm Marilyn Cross, and what firm are you all with?" she asks with a huge smile.

I am on the couch and say nothing at all, but can't believe my ears and eyes. I don't want to screw up whatever plan they have worked out, so I just look and smile.

Hatch has made his way into the kitchen and is listening to the play-out in the living room, stick at the ready, in case one of them comes within striking distance.

"You can't just walk in here and look around like this!" Frank says.

"I have a cleared appointment here today with the owner who put this property in the hands of Big Buy. I have every right to be here and sell this property!"

"Come on, Honey, let's look around!" Lil says, grabbing Pali's hand, and they make their way into the dining room.

"What the hell's going on here, Frank?" one of the guys says.

"I don't know. Just let them look around, and then they'll leave. We'll finish later," he says quietly.

Frank looks over at me, and I make no facial expression at all. Out of the corner of my eye, I saw Hatch peek out from the kitchen and nod to me.

As Pali and Lil are touring the dining room, Pali picks up a heavy glass vase and puts his hands behind his back, holding it, just waiting for an opportunity to crack one of the guys over the head with it.

Frank crosses the room, puts his back to the kitchen door, and with that Hatch comes down on him with the stick, dropping him to the floor in one blow. When Pali sees that, he cracks one of the other two across the skull with the vase, dropping him.

Edna and Lil pounce on the remaining guy and hold him down.

"There's a roll of duct tape in the kitchen!" I say and leap over Frank, lying in the doorway, and grab it.

"Roll him over, roll him over!" Lil yells. "We'll duct tape his hands and feet."

Edna and Lil roll the guy over, while he yells his head off, but they hold him down, and I wrap his feet first and then his hands and he is incapacitated.

"Put a piece on that mouth!" says Edna. "I'm tired of hearing all those obscenities he's yelling. My, my, do you talk to your mother with that mouth? My, my!"

Frank and the other guy are still out cold, so we duct tape them as well, just in case they come to.

"Let's get out of here," says Hatch and takes me by the hand. "You okay, Babs?" he asks, looking at me with concern.

"I'm great! Let's go."

We start out the front door, much relieved, when the black sedan rolls back into the driveway.

"Oh shit!" yells Pali, and we all run inside again. Now there are two guys rather than just the driver, and the extra guy is Chuck Mahan. They see us and get out of the car and run to the porch. We lock the door, but in two minutes, the driver pulls out a pistol and starts shooting the lock off.

We all run, leaping over Frank Sallman still lying in the kitchen doorway, and out the back door. We run as hard as we can and get to the woods. Hatch and I are in the lead with Pali right behind, Edna and Lil are bringing up the rear.

"I'm too fat to run this fast!" yells Edna.

One shot sails past us and Lil says, "Not me," and charges past all of us.

Several downed trees are piled up and Hatch and I jump behind them, the other three following. The driver unloads his gun into the woods, evidently only hitting trees, because we are all safe. Scared, but safe.

We aren't twenty feet from them and can see all of their actions. Now out of ammunition, they aren't sure just what to do. Chuck Mahan and the guy are arguing, and it's clear they have no idea what to do next. In the near distance, we hear a siren. Hopefully the North East Police Department has finally pulled together and arrived. Chuck and the driver look around. The driver throws his gun into the woods just as the police call out, "Freeze! Don't take another step!" They both freeze.

Once the officers has them still and handcuffed. We all come out of the woods. Chief Evans is one of the policemen and isn't surprised to see us here.

"Scotty had a meltdown—quite possibly a nervous breakdown—spilling the beans to everybody at the shop, and they called us."

"You'll find Frank Sallman and two others tied up inside," says Hatch.

Chuck Mahan is crying now, saying he can't lose all of that money, his wife will kill him, and he hates Richard Mallor for screwing up all of his plans.

Epilogue

The weatherman says muggy, but a breeze has kicked up out of the west and turned this night into a warm, breezy evening with clear skies that contain more stars than I've ever seen. Maybe it is the location of Edna and Al's place out on a private road on the outskirts of town with little traffic and complete privacy. Al has cooked on the grill, we've all brought food and drinks, and it is just us. Pali and Ethel, Edna and Al, Lil, Hatch, and me. We eat and have a few beers and wine while sitting around a small campfire that Al has prepared. It lends atmosphere to the evening and keeps the mosquitoes at bay— it is June and they are making their yearly presence known early this year.

Lil is about half shot and breaks out in almost uncontrollable laughter. Once recovered enough to talk, she says, "Remember when that guy came running into the body shop all full of gasoline and all sweaty, telling us there was a crazy man threatening to set him on fire if he didn't tell him where Annie was?"

"Yeah, and he almost collapsed when Pali jumped up and grabbed him, saying he'd smash his head on the counter if he didn't tell us where she was? The look on his face was of complete horror and priceless!" Edna says, laughing, too.

"I don't know how I planned to do that, since he outweighed me by about one hundred pounds or so," Pali adds, and we all laugh again.

"That was a great night, the most excitement I've had ever . . . well, with my clothes on!" Lil ends.

"That did it. Who needs another beer?" Al asks.

"Not Hatch," I say, smiling.

"Don't *you* talk. Hide any wine you might have, Al," he says, pointing at me.

Pali and Ethel are snuggling on a glider and talking quietly, and I envy their closeness. Lots of memories, a lifetime together. Edna and Al are retrieving more beer, and Lil announces that she has to find a potty.

"Let's walk in the moonlight, Annie," Hatch says.

"I'd like that."

The moon is full and illuminates everything. We walk down the driveway and up the road, making our way to a small stone bridge we crossed coming here, and I can hear the babble of water rushing over stones. He looks at me and I glance back just as he takes my hand, pulling me into him. Backing me up against the stone wall of the bridge, he puts one hand on the side of my head, running his thumb lightly across my lips while the other hand is around my waist. He kisses me like I've never been kissed before. A deep and sensuous kiss that lasts long and leaves me limp, but is all I ever hoped it would be.

The End

CPSIA information can be obtained at www.ICGtesting.com
Printed in the USA
BVOW03s0202200614

356922BV00001B/6/P

9 781631 351587